I was secure
enough to admit
that the
thyss-cub was
significantly
cuter than me.

TOM O'DONNELL

razOr
bill

An Imprint of Penguin Group (USA)

razOr
bill

A division of Penguin Young Readers Group
Published by the Penguin Group
Penguin Group (USA) LLC
345 Hudson Street
New York, New York 10014

USA / Canada / UK / Ireland / Australia / New Zealand / India / South Africa / China
Penguin.com
A Penguin Random House Company

ISBN: 978-1-59514-713-4

Printed in the United States of America

1 3 5 7 9 10 8 6 4 2

CHAPTER ONE

I crouched, motionless, and watched the alien invaders in the canyon below. There were four of them, and they were hideous. Each had four long appendages radiating from a central trunk. On top of their bodies sat wobbly round heads with two slimy-looking eyes stuck right in the middle. And on top of each head was a ridiculous tuft of colored fur!

I was only a few dozen meters away. It was the first time I'd seen the aliens.

They had invaded Gelo two months ago. Their huge ship had dropped from the sky in a cloud of fire brighter than the sun. They landed, and almost immediately they began to dig.

Terrified, I had asked Kalac, my originator, where the space invaders came from.

"They come from Eo," it replied.

"You mean that little blue dot between us and the sun?" I asked, thinking back to astronomy instruction. Kalac nodded. That dot didn't seem impressive enough to be the home of an evil alien empire. T'utzuxe the Red Planet, I could believe. But not Eo.

"There are billions of them there," said Kalac.

Well, I guess their home planet didn't have enough iridium for all of them, because they sure wanted ours. Day and night, they drilled huge holes toward the core of our asteroid. Their oversized vehicles rumbled to and fro. Into the tunnel, empty. Out of the tunnel, heavy with ore. It seemed like they meant to take it all.

The one good thing about this particular alien invasion was that the aliens didn't seem to know they'd invaded anyone at all. They'd been mining our asteroid for two months and they weren't even aware of our existence.

We watched them from the shadows. We examined whatever they left behind. We eavesdropped on their radio transmissions from the safety of our tunnels and tried to make sense of their strange language.

The fact that we had not been detected was not just due to the unobservant nature of their species. It was also because we Xotonians are very, very good at hiding. For starters, each of us possesses the innate ability to change the color of our skin at will—perfect for camouflage.

In fact, at that very moment, I had turned myself a dull shade of blue-gray (the same exact blue-gray of everything on the surface of Gelo). I was hiding, more or less in plain sight, from the four "humans."

Yes, that is what they called themselves: humans. Two months of secretly listening to them talk to one another on their radios, and we'd at least figured out their name for their own species.

Honestly, I had not come to this place expecting to see any humans at all. After much pleading, Kalac had finally allowed me to go on a "reconnaissance mission" to the surface, to a canyon called Jehe, a few kilometers from where the human mothership had landed.

It was an area where no one had seen any humans, and no one expected to. I was simply to check the area for their garbage—which they tended to leave everywhere they went—and make sure that Jehe Canyon was still human-free. Indeed, if I saw any actual humans, I was to return home immediately to avoid the possibility of detection. No exceptions.

Some might have considered this a menial or even useless task, but not me. I was excited to finally get a chance to do my part, however small, for the Xotonian cause. I was desperate to show Kalac—and everyone else, for that matter—that I could do a good job, that I could handle responsibility. It was on my sixth tour of this garbage-free canyon that I suddenly saw four specks on the horizon. Actual humans.

At this point, I should have returned home to avoid the possibility of detection. But I didn't. I couldn't. I just had to see the humans for myself. So I hid among the rocks.

The humans approached with astounding speed, each riding on a small rocket-propelled vehicle. We Xotonians have nothing like these rockets. The fastest we move is when we run or occasionally ride an usk-lizard.

They pulled up to Jehe Canyon in a cloud of exhaust: two "males" and two "females." Kalac had tried to explain the concept of human "gender" to me once, but I still couldn't quite wrap my brain around it. Apparently, the human population was equally divided between two sub-species possessing minor physical differences. These differences were not always apparent to our Xotonian scouts. So the Council had to come up with a quick rule for telling the two apart: Often (but not always) the female humans have longer head-fur than the males. But male humans have more fur overall. Aliens are weird.

My initial observation on seeing these four specimens:

They were smaller than I expected. I'd been told that the average human is between 150 and 190 centimeters tall, a giant by Xotonian standards. But the shortest of these was barely 130 centimeters (about my height).

Each of them was encased in a shiny coating with a transparent helmet over their heads. The elders said they couldn't breathe the atmosphere on Gelo's surface, so they had to bring their own Eo air with them. Why go somewhere you can't breathe? I wondered. In my experience, breathing is one of the most important things.

Once they were in Jehe Canyon, the four humans began to fly to and fro on their personal rockets. These vehicles had a sort of saddle around which the humans wrapped their lower appendages and a pronged steering mechanism that they gripped and turned with their upper appendages. They were capable of very tight maneuvers. Was I witnessing some sort of military exercise? Were these humans practicing tactics that they might eventually use against my own people?

Sometimes they would talk among themselves via communicators inside their helmets. I listened in as best as I could with my Nyrt-Snooper.

The Nyrt-Snooper is another classic example of Xotonian sneakiness. It is a tiny device that fits in a Xotonian ear cavity and allows us to secretly listen in on radio transmissions.

There are only thirty-one Nyrt-Snoopers in existence on all of Gelo, so I considered it quite an honor that I had been given the use of one for this mission (even if it was staticky and had a little bit of earwax on it from the last Xotonian). Though I couldn't understand a word of human, I wanted to determine their command order and build a profile of each of them. You know, reconnaissance stuff!

Let me begin by describing the largest human of the group. The brownish head-fur was cropped close to the head, so I pegged him for a male. He had the deepest voice of all four. But his voice would occasionally crackle into a very high register, seemingly at random. Quite disturbing. From what I could tell, he seemed to be the leader of the group.

Next there were the two medium-sized female duplicates. I say "duplicates" because in all respects they appeared to be exact copies of one another: same long black head-fur, same build; even their voices were alike. The only difference I could see were the transparent glass-and-plastic lenses one of them wore over her brown eyes. Perhaps this was simply a courtesy so that others could tell them apart?

As physically similar as the duplicates were, they seemed to be different in temperament. The duplicate without the lenses (whom I will call "No-Lenses") seemed to challenge the authority of the large male (whom I will call "Crackle-

Voice") at every turn. Meanwhile, the other duplicate (whom I will call "Lenses") was more docile and quiet. Lenses seemed to quickly lose interest in swerving around on the rockets. She soon abandoned hers and sat down on a rock to watch the others.

Now to the smallest, and perhaps the most puzzling, of the humans. He was male and a full thirty centimeters shorter than the duplicates, with a wild puff of bright red head-fur (or maybe plumage?). Unlike the others, he seemed to constantly be falling off his rocket—marked with considerably more dents and scratches than those of his comrades—and landing in the blue-gray Gelo dust.

Whenever these tumbles happened, Red-Fur would hop right back up, making a peculiar gurgling barking sound. Then he would get on his rocket and try again. Usually with the same result.

Once, after making sure he had the full attention of the other three, Red-Fur attempted to fly his rocket through the narrow gap between two big, standing boulders. He backed up and then blasted off.

But the space between the rocks wasn't wide enough. Red-Fur hit the gap, but his rocket got stuck fast. Unfortunately for him, he kept going. Red-Fur flew at least ten meters through the air, then skidded another ten on his head.

He lay on the ground, motionless. I wondered if he had been squished to goo inside his shiny encasement suit. All the other humans stared at each other in silence. Then, once again, that familiar barking sound over the communicator. Red-Fur arose, apparently unhurt.

"Yoo-gize-toe-duh-lee-thott-i-wuzz-dedd," he chirped over the radio.

"Nott-funn-ee," replied Lenses.

"Kine-duh-funn-ee," said Red-Fur. Pure human gibberish. I couldn't understand one bit.

After spending a good ten minutes helping unstick Red-Fur's rocket from between the boulders, Crackle-Voice and No-Lenses pulled the nose-cones of their own rockets into alignment. Then they started to point out various landmarks in the canyon and talk via their communicators. That's when it dawned on me. They were going to race!

Lenses was summoned from her rock to be the judge of the outcome. She stood between the two rockets, holding her two upper appendages high. Then she called a single human word: "Go!"

The rockets were off! Crackle-Voice and No-Lenses blasted forward with a deafening boom. From what I could tell, they were traveling twice as fast as I had seen these small rockets go before. The two racers kept nose-and-nose as they traced the crescent curve of Jehe Canyon. White smoke and blue dust billowed behind them. Even Red-Fur, whose attention certainly seemed fleeting, watched the race intently.

The rockets swerved to dodge rocks and craters and avoid the ever-shifting walls of the canyon on either side. They must have been going 150 kilometers per hour, but somehow they stayed neck-and-neck with each other. There was barely any space between them, and I couldn't tell who was winning.

At the far end of the canyon, they rounded a wide crater: the halfway point of the race. Crackle-Voice cut the curve a little sharper and grabbed a clear lead. No-Lenses leaned forward on her rocket, trying to catch up.

They were in the home stretch now, flames exploding from their thrusters. No-Lenses was about one rocket-length behind, and she couldn't seem to make up any lost ground. Crackle-Voice was going to win.

All of a sudden, with less than three hundred meters to go, No-Lenses swerved off to the right. What was she doing? Had she just given up and conceded victory? Even Crackle-Voice turned back to look.

No-Lenses flew straight for the two standing boulders— the very gap where Red-Fur's rocket had gotten stuck!

Then I understood her plan: If she could somehow squeeze between them, the distance between her and the finish line would be cut in half.

But there was no way she could squeeze between them! There just wasn't enough space. And No-Lenses was flying twice as fast as Red-Fur had been. I shuddered to imagine the aftermath of a wreck like that: She would surely be killed!

Wait a second. Why should I care if No-Lenses got smashed to bits in a rocket race? It would be a good thing. One less alien invader for us to deal with.

Still, my is'pog was beating fast, and I couldn't look away. Neither could Lenses or Red-Fur, who both stood mesmerized at the finish line.

No-Lenses was flying fast toward the gap, only a few meters away now. At the last possible moment, she leaned right while rotating the rocket sideways to the left. Could she somehow narrow the rocket's width by putting it on its side? No-Lenses hit the gap with the squeal of metal scraping against rock. Sparks flew and—

Somehow she came flying out the other side! Victory! No-Lenses finished just ahead of Crackle-Voice. I wanted to cheer, but I held my gul'orp. Red-Fur leaped into the air. Lenses just shook her head.

Slowly, Crackle-Voice climbed down off his rocket and

approached No-Lenses. Crackle-Voice, apparently the group's leader, had just been defeated by a subordinate in front of others. Totally humiliated. Now they will fight, I thought.

The two humans stood staring at each other for a moment. At last Crackle-Voice extended one of his upper appendages. No-Lenses took it in her grasper, and they shook. Both began that weird human barking noise. Red-Fur joined in too.

That was when it dawned on me. All the barking and the teeth-baring expression that accompanied it: It was laughter! When Xotonians laugh, we make a loud metallic honking noise (naturally). I hadn't even considered what the human version might sound like. Or even that humans could laugh at all.

But if these four were laughing so much, then flying their rockets through Jehe Canyon probably wasn't a military exercise at all. They were just goofing around and having fun.

Crackle-Voice, No-Lenses, and Red-Fur spent the next ten minutes excitedly reliving the race. Eventually, all three hopped on their rockets and flew to the gap in the boulders. No-Lenses proceeded to teach them the trick of turning the rocket sideways to pass through the narrow space.

Lenses didn't join them, however. She sat back down on her rock and pulled a shiny black rectangle out onto her lap. With a flick of her grasper, the device lit up. Suddenly, a 3-D holographic projection was swimming in the air above the device.

We Xotonians have computers, but they were nothing like this. The display was beautiful. Shimmering and sparkling with bright blues and warm pinks. I give the alien invaders credit where it is due: They are light-years beyond my people in graphic design.

I couldn't help myself. I silently crept within a few meters of Lenses for a better look.

By swiping her upper appendage through the holographic space, she seemed to be navigating some sort of computer interface. Glowing icons zoomed past until at last she found the one she wanted. She reached up with her grasper and poked it.

Suddenly, the hologram projection showed the stars. Red-and-green ringed planets spun slowly in the distance. Farther out were glowing nebulae and rotating spiral galaxies. A comet sailed past.

In front of Lenses, a glowing, holographic blaster weapon hovered in the air, the handle toward her. She grabbed it. With her other appendage she punched a virtual green button at the bottom of the projection. And just like that, she was in the middle of a war.

Saucer-shaped ships hurtled toward her from space. With her blaster, she fired angry bolts of red energy at them. When the spacecraft were hit, they would trail flame and exhaust and sometimes spiral out of control. Occasionally, one would explode in a halo of metal and fire. This human female was repelling an alien invasion!

Faster and faster the alien saucers came. When they got past her shield barriers, the whole projection would flash red, and a glowing meter at the top of the display would shrink. But she was good. For every ten that came at her, she shot down nine. At last, the meter shrank to nothing. The whole projection froze and faded to gray.

And then she started the invasion all over again. It was just some sort of simulation. Realistic and thrilling, but completely imaginary.

Lenses repeated the scenario at least ten times. I must say, it looked really, really fun. Watching her play almost made me wish my home had been invaded by aliens. Then I remembered that it had.

By this time, the other humans had all mastered No-Lenses's rolling-sideways rocket trick. They were sailing through the gap, two at a time.

At last they came back and tried to persuade Lenses to give the new boulder trick a try. After a little coaxing, she gave in. Lenses deactivated the holographic simulation and hopped back on her rocket to join them.

Part of me wanted to watch these humans forever. Something about how they interacted was fascinating. Very un-Xotonian, in a way that I just couldn't put my thol'graz on. I almost wished I was out there on a fifth rocket, blasting around and laughing along with them.

But no. These aliens were part of an invading army that came from the stars to steal our iridium.

Plus they had only two eyes. Two eyes! The very thought made my skin crawl. Why two? Everyone knows you need at least three. And, of course, five is the best number of eyes to have.

T'utzuxe was slipping below the horizon, and the sun was soon to follow. I checked my chronometer. Only an hour until the Grand Conclave at Core-of-Rock. It was time for me to leave.

I had completed my reconnaissance mission: There were four undersized humans in Jehe Canyon, wasting time on rockets. Not a threat.

I turned to go. As I did, something glinted on the rocks below. It was the shiny black rectangle, the hologram projector device. Lenses had left it behind.

Disobeying Kalac's order to return home immediately

upon seeing humans was arguably forgivable. After all, they hadn't detected me, so what was the harm? But what I did next would be harder to defend.

When I was sure the four humans were thoroughly distracted, I took the device.

CHAPTER TWO

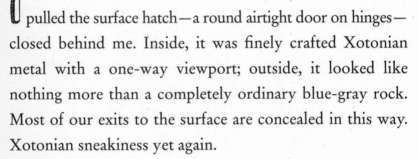

I pulled the surface hatch—a round airtight door on hinges—closed behind me. Inside, it was finely crafted Xotonian metal with a one-way viewport; outside, it looked like nothing more than a completely ordinary blue-gray rock. Most of our exits to the surface are concealed in this way. Xotonian sneakiness yet again.

I started back toward Core-of-Rock, clutching the holographic projector in my thol'graz.

I wouldn't say this to Kalac, but the surface of our asteroid is, quite frankly, boring—a whole lot of craters and dust. To experience the real Gelo, you must dig a bit deeper. Our asteroid is riddled with tunnels. Though no one can say with absolute certainty, the elders believe that the core is probably more tunnel than not. And when I say "tunnels," I don't mean the new human mines. Those are just crude rectangular holes. I mean the ancient, endless tunnels. A twisting cavern system so vast that much of it remains unexplored, even by Xotonians. Our chief worry was that the human miners would accidentally dig their way into these tunnels and discover the Xotonian race. By all accounts they were getting closer every day.

Tunnels may not sound exciting to you. But you must understand that Xotonians are not the only creatures that live beneath the surface of Gelo. My people only inhabit roughly 2 percent of the total cavern system of Gelo. The rest is wilderness. It is what we call the Unclaimed Tunnels.

In the Unclaimed Tunnels, there are towering forests of giant fungi and fields of luminous mushrooms. There are bottomless lakes teeming with schools of blind r'yaris and who knows what other creatures. There are chambers so wide and tall that it is impossible to say where they begin or end. Herds of wild usk-lizards gallop across these underground plains, and deadly thyss-cats stalk them.

Ours is a whole subterranean ecosystem, as distinct from the surface as could be. Even the air is different down here. Xotonians can breathe the thin atmosphere of Gelo's surface, but not as easily as the oxygen-rich air of the cavern system below.

I wound my way through the tunnels, mentally reversing

the twenty-seven turns it had taken me to get from Core-of-Rock to the surface entrance near Jehe Canyon. Twenty-seven turns might sound like a lot to remember, but when you live your life in a cavern system, you need to have an excellent memory (as all Xotonians do).

At last the tunnel widened, and I came to the formal boundary between the Unclaimed Tunnels and the Xotonian city: a shimmering field of purple energy swimming in the air before me. Our Stealth Shield.

The shield was created by our ancestors long ago. It completely envelops our underground city and conceals it from outside scanners and sensors. It was also the main reason the humans hadn't detected us yet. When they had observed the asteroid from Eo with their telescopes and orbital satellites and other instruments, the Stealth Shield had sent back false information. To the human computers, our city appeared to be nothing more than solid rock. Even our ancestors were sneaky.

I felt a slight tingle on my skin as I stepped through the shield. Behind it, the tunnel opened onto a huge domed chamber, a few kilometers across. The light of thousands of Xotonian dwellings twinkled in the gloom. This was the city of Core-of-Rock—my home.

On the outskirts of Core-of-Rock, I passed farms.

Fields of mushrooms grew in straight rows, and dull-eyed usk-lizards grazed on lichen. No farmers, though. They had already headed into town. The Grand Conclave was about to begin.

Soon, the singular mass of the city began to resolve itself into individual buildings. They were mostly low and round with the occasional tower poking up above its neighbors like an oversized stalagmite. Even at a distance, a few structures stood out clearly among the others: the Hall of Wonok, our center of government, stately and imposing; the dull gray pyramid of the Vault, at once mysterious and forgettable; and Dynusk's Column, our center of observation, spiraling all the way up to the ceiling of the chamber high above.

My family's dwelling stood closer to the center of the city. The houses here were a tight-packed jumble, nearly touching one another. After a quick detour to my chamber—where I stashed the hologram device under my sleeping-veth—I made my way toward Ryzz Plaza.

Ryzz Plaza was the social hub of our society, a bit of open space in the very densest part of Core-of-Rock. In the middle of it stood an iridium statue of Great Jalasu Jhuk, striking a heroic pose, one thol'graz extended, as if pointing the way toward the future. At the base of the Great Progenitor's statue stood the less-than-epic leaders of my own

19

time. Four members of the Xotonian Council, in the flesh: Loghoz, Dyves, Glyac, and Sheln.

Normally, a Council meeting would take place inside the Hall of Wonok. But a Grand Conclave is no normal Council meeting, and the hall was far too small to accommodate it. Thousands of Xotonians, young and old, had already gathered in the plaza, and more were still filing in. Some wore the drab breechcloths or rough-spun tunics of laborers; others the sparkling x'yzoth jewelry and bright feathered cloaks of the elite; still others the usk-leather helmets and cuirasses of the city guard. Every stratum of our small society—from Ydar, the High Observer, to several well-known professional oog-ball players, to Sertor, who runs a food stall in the market—had turned out. The whole population of Core-of-Rock was here in one place.

"Hey, Chorkle! What's the good word?" someone yelled out from the crowd. I turned.

There stood Hudka, my grand-originator, leaning on a cane. Hudka was so old and stooped, it was barely taller than me.

"Hudka!" I cried, and hugged it.

"Careful, don't break me, Chorkle," it said, but it hugged back just as hard. "So are you ready to listen to a whole load of nonsense?"

"This is important," I said. "We have to decide what to do about the humans." A Grand Conclave was an extremely rare event, and I was excited.

"Eh. They mainly call Conclaves to hear themselves flap their own gul'orps for a while before a bad decision is made," said Hudka. "The Council is a pack of idiots! Possibly dumber than the population at large. And I should know, I was on the Council! I've sat through quite a few Conclaves, and I can tell you with certainty: I'd rather be having dental work done."

"You must have been on the Council a really long time ago," I said. "Had the Big Bang happened yet?"

"You know, when I finally pass to the Nebula Beyond," chuckled Hudka, "you won't be able to make fun of me for being old anymore. What are you gonna do with all your spare time?"

"Make fun of you for being dead?" I said. Hudka laughed.

Now this may sound harsh to the outside observer, but Hudka and I always teased each other. It's hard to explain, but it was just part of the relationship we had.

Hudka squinted. "Well, look at that," it said, shaking its head. "Here comes the biggest gul'orp-flapper of them all!"

At the center of the plaza, under Jalasu Jhuk's resolute

gaze, the Chief of the Council joined the other four members. This was Kalac, Hudka's offspring and my originator.

Yes, I was the direct offspring of the elected leader of the Xotonian people. You might think this would mean countless perks and advantages for me. Mostly it was just awkward. I was proud of Kalac, but it seemed I could never quite measure up to its great deeds. And I often felt like I was judged twice as harshly for my own mistakes—which somehow seemed to occur more frequently the older I got. Anything I did, good or bad, was also a reflection on the Chief of the Council's leadership. Other Xotonians couldn't understand how a strong, dynamic figure like Kalac could have such an odd, quiet (often scatterbrained) offspring like me.

But I wasn't the only one who didn't have the smoothest relationship with Kalac. As far back as I could remember, Hudka and Kalac had been at odds. This conflict was only heightened by the fact that Hudka lived with us.

At this point, all the Council members had arrived, and the Conclave was called to order.

"By Great Jalasu Jhuk of the Stars," cried Loghoz, the Custodian of the Council. "Let this, the eight hundred seventeenth Grand Conclave of the Xotonian people, commence! The first to speak will be Council Member Sheln!" A hush fell over the plaza.

Sheln, a heavyset, dull-eyed Xotonian, stepped forward. It had recently challenged Kalac for the position of Chief of the Council and lost the vote. To put it mildly, I knew that Kalac didn't have the highest opinion of Sheln's intelligence or integrity.

"We all know why we're gathered here today," said Sheln, gesturing broadly with its upper thol'grazes and stroking its z'iuk with its lower ones. "Because of them!" Sheln pointed ominously at the roof of the chamber, toward the surface of the asteroid. The crowd shuddered, and many squealed in fright. Few had laid eyes on a human, so whatever they were imagining could only be more frightening than reality.

"The so-called hoo-mins," said Sheln, mispronouncing the word. "They have invaded our homeland. Day and night their machines rumble. Spewing exhaust. Throwing out garbage everywhere. Digging deeper and deeper into our world. And for what?"

Sheln produced a small chunk of shiny metal. It tossed the little nugget up and down a few times, then continued. "Iridium. They came to steal it. Now I don't need to tell you folks, but we Xotonians need iridium for power. If the hoo-mins take it all, then guess what? No more electricity. No more Stealth Shield. It'll be lights out for us."

Sheln suddenly pocketed the iridium lump.

"Some may say, 'Oh, but once the nice hoo-mins get enough iridium, they'll simply leave and go back to Eo,'" said Sheln, affecting a simpering tone. "Well, they've got a whole planet, ten times the size of our asteroid, and that still wasn't enough for them! Hoo-min greed and aggression know no bounds. This goes deeper than iridium, folks. This is about right and wrong. This is about good and evil. This is about the very future of the Xotonian race. These hoo-mins, they hate our way of life."

At this, the crowd quaked with dread. Many began to weep openly, big, salty tears dripping from all five eyes. With large groups of Xotonians, emotions tend to run high.

"How can they hate our way of life if they don't know we exist?" called out Hudka. The collective sobbing of the Conclave was undercut by a ripple of nervous laughter.

"Hudka? Is that you, you old bag of spores?" cried Sheln, scanning the crowd. "You're a hundred years into senility. Why don't you shut your stupid gul'orp and leave this to the Council?"

"You're right. It took me a long time to go senile," cried Hudka. "I defer to one who achieved it at such a young age."

The crowd laughed louder this time. A few even clapped.

24

"I'm not the one who's . . . who are you calling . . . I'm street smart!" Sheln sputtered with rage.

"Order! We must have order at the Conclave," called Loghoz, still dabbing its eyes with the corner of its cloak.

"Now is not the time, Hudka," said Kalac firmly. Hudka shrugged and gestured for Sheln to continue.

"The point," growled Sheln, "is that whether certain appeasers admit it or not, we are at war." Sheln paused to let that final word sink in for a little while.

"But by Great Jalasu Jhuk, this is a war we can win!" cried Sheln. "Human technology is pathetic. They still use combustion-based projectile weapons! We have energy blasters—two hundred fifty-six of them, in fact. All in good working order. We have seventeen personal shield devices. They have none. We can monitor and jam their radio communications with our Nyrt-Snoopers. And let us not forget, folks, we have the Q-sik." Sheln gestured toward the Vault, which sat behind Ryzz Plaza. It was a bold move to mention the legendary Xotonian weapon. Perhaps too bold?

"Plus we have the element of surprise," continued Sheln. "But not forever. Estimates put the hoo-mins only twenty-one days away from tunneling right into the Gelo cavern system. Once that happens, they'll figure out we're here. We'll lose the advantage.

"That is why we must strike now! A small group of Xotonian warriors should take the Q-sik and blast the hoo-min spacecraft while they sleep. Boom! If any of them manage to make it out of their ship, we pick them off one at a time with our blasters. Pow, pow, pow! A single battle, and the war is over. Xotonians win."

It sounded more like a slaughter than a battle to me. I imagined the four humans I'd seen, disintegrated by the Q-sik or shot down as they fled their burning home. The crowd murmured in excitement or fear or both. Sheln had certainly painted a vivid picture.

"Next to address the Conclave will be Kalac, the Chief of the Council," said Loghoz.

Kalac stepped forward. "I agree with certain points my fellow Council member has made," said Kalac, gesturing to Sheln. "The humans are a threat to us. About that, there can be no doubt."

Sheln nodded. Kalac continued.

"But war is serious business. In considering the possibility, we cannot only name our advantages. We must take honest stock of our disadvantages as well. The first of those is numbers. There are twelve billion humans back on Eo. I'll say it again: twelve billion. By comparison, there are about six thousand Xotonians. So it doesn't matter how good our blasters are when compared with their guns. They outnumber us roughly two million to one."

At this terrifying statistic, the crowd broke down again—loud bawling, howls of terror; some even fell and began to pound the cavern floor in despair.

"Yes, there are at least two hundred million kilometers between us and most of them," continued Kalac, "but this only highlights a second disadvantage we have: space travel. We all know that in the Time of Legends the Xotonian race could travel the stars as easily as we walk between caverns today. But those days are long behind us. The humans have spacecraft. We don't. That means that even if we defeat them, they can just come back again. And again.

"So I propose to you all an alternate plan. One that preserves our advantage of surprise entirely," said Kalac. "Let us attack the humans without attacking them." There was a buzz of general confusion as the crowd tried to pull itself back together.

"Pardon me, Kalac," said Loghoz, "but that is a logical contradiction."

"Perhaps it would be better if I showed you what I mean," said Kalac, and it wheeled forward a view-screen large enough for even those in the back of the crowd to see. Kalac activated the screen. It showed a green map depicting a well-known part of the cavern system. I couldn't help but notice how shabby the Xotonian display looked compared with the human hologram device.

"This is an area of the Gelo caverns," said Kalac. "And these are the mines that the humans have dug." It clicked the view-screen remote. Now the mines, square shafts shown in yellow, were overlaid upon the twisting caverns. At several points the yellow and green were nearly touching.

"But by destroying supports here," said Kalac, indicating a point on the map, "we could cause a major subterranean collapse. Both the human mines and the natural caverns below them would fall in on themselves. On the surface, this would result in a major asteroid-quake." Now the map showed the zone of collapse shaded in purple, completely inscribing the mines and caverns.

"This would happen right beneath the human mothership," said Kalac. It clicked again, and now the outline of the grounded human vessel sat squarely in the middle of the purple zone. The crowd gasped and began to whisper among themselves.

"This collapse would damage the human spacecraft, perhaps critically, and destroy much of their mining equipment. Best of all, the humans would believe it was simply a natural disaster," said Kalac. "They would never even know that any Xotonians were involved."

"Just a moment," said Dyves, another member of the Council. "Those 'supports' you pointed out are kilometers of solid rock. Destroying them would be impossible. Simply impossible."

Kalac paused. "Not if we use the Q-sik." Another murmur rumbled through the crowd.

"From the time of Jalasu Jhuk," said Kalac, "each Chief of the Council has been passed down an eight-digit numeric code. This is the code to open the Vault. I know that to some of you, using the Q-sik may seem brash, or even sacrilegious. But we face an unprecedented emergency. I believe we can remove the device, use it just once, and then return it to its rightful place."

"But what's to stop the humans from returning?" asked Glyac, the fifth member of the Council. Up to this point, the casual observer would be forgiven for wondering whether Glyac was awake or not.

"What will stop them," said Kalac, "is themselves. If we attack the humans directly, even if we win, they are certain to come back in force. We've observed them enough to understand that retaliation is in their nature." Sheln grumbled and shook its head.

Kalac continued, "But if a 'natural disaster' destroys their settlement, well, the humans will conclude that asteroid mining is too unsafe to pursue any further. And even if they return, they will pick a different asteroid to mine. After all, there are millions of others in the solar system. Presumably with just as much iridium."

I could tell the crowd was coming around to Kalac's way of thinking. Hudka still wasn't convinced, though.

"Doing nothing is not an option," said Kalac. "The humans show no sign of leaving. Starting an open war with them is not an option either. We'll lose. Using the Q-sik to create an asteroid-quake is the only way to avert disaster."

Kalac had made its case. It was done. And maybe it was right? Maybe the humans would declare their invasion a bust and go back to their little blue dot. I felt a sudden pang at the thought of the four laughing humans leaving our asteroid forever.

No, I told myself, they're just a bunch of gross two-eyed space invaders who don't even belong here! Good riddance. Right?

"Does the Council," said Loghoz, "wish to propose any other—"

"Yup! Over here, kid!" cried Hudka. Loghoz sank when it realized who was speaking.

All eyes were now on us. I shrank from the attention.

My grand-originator is a remarkable Xotonian, but it can also be an embarrassing one.

Most believe that Hudka is the oldest living member of our race, though there is some debate on this point. Gatas always claimed that it was three days older, but Hudka disagreed. Strongly. Gatas had effectively lost the argument a while back, when it went completely deaf and could no longer hold its own in shouting matches with my grand-originator.

Xotonians generally give Hudka a bit of respect for its advanced age. Hudka calls this the "not-dead-yet factor." But it has never been in Hudka's nature to tell others what they want to hear. And when you've been that outspoken for that long in a community as small as ours, you've already given everyone you've ever met several doses of opinion. In many ways, Hudka was now just a small, wrinkled vessel for opinions. And the older Hudka got, the louder those opinions became.

"Hudka, please," said Loghoz, sighing.

"Don't you try to get high-thol'grazed with me, Loghoz. I was on the Council when you were still an egg sac!" said Hudka. Loghoz blinked.

I looked to Kalac. My originator was straining to keep calm.

"Hudka, you are no longer a Council member," said Kalac in an overly measured tone. "We cannot have every—"

"Aw, not this one again," said Hudka to the crowd. "Kalac, didn't you just blather on for an hour? I wouldn't know. I think I fell asleep right after you started talking!"

Nervous laughter from the crowd. They were torn. A lot of them thought Hudka was a nutty old crank, but the spirit of a Conclave is democratic. Anyone who has an idea should be able to share it.

"If the Council agrees, Hudka may address the Conclave," said Loghoz at last. "All in favor?"

Four thol'grazes went up—three grudgingly. Only Sheln seemed particularly eager to hear Hudka out. It clearly just wanted Kalac to be publicly embarrassed by its own originator.

"All opposed?"

Only one thol'graz. Kalac's, of course.

"By a vote of four to one, the Council resolves to allow Hudka to address the Conclave," said Loghoz. "But please, Hudka, try to keep it brief and to the point."

"Thank you, Loghoz. You're smarter than you look, and don't ever let anybody tell you different," said Hudka. Loghoz blinked again.

"First off," said Hudka, enjoying the attention, "iridium."

Suddenly Sheln was the one who looked nervous.

"This mushroom-head had the cergs to stand up here in front of all of you and say that the humans are going to take all of our iridium and leave us poor Xotonians without power," said Hudka, pointing right at Sheln. "Guano!

"If you know anything about science—which I'll grant that most of you folks don't—you'd understand that this much iridium"—Hudka held two brips the barest width apart—"is enough to power our entire city for a whole year! Such was the genius of the technology our great ancestors created. I personally have enough iridium in my closet to keep us in power for ten million years. Even I'll be dead by then!

"Fact is, there's ample iridium for Xotonian and human both. Iridium's not the issue," said Hudka definitively. At this point Sheln had turned nearly plaid with anger.

From what I understood, Hudka was right. The ancient reactor that powered all of Core-of-Rock was incredibly efficient. It only required a tiny amount of iridium to keep running.

"Second: attacking the humans," said Hudka. "Both of these so-called plans the Council has presented are just attacking the humans. One's a direct attack. The other's a sneak attack. Same difference. Folks will get hurt, maybe even die. I ask all of you why we would attack before we've been attacked? Is this the Xotonian way? To strike first and ask questions later? That's not what we tell our younglings to do. That's not what we should do. All of you who want to rush to violence should be ashamed of yourselves."

Sheln sure didn't look ashamed. Kalac didn't either.

"Now I'll grant you that these humans could turn out to be tough customers. They sure are ugly, so they might be mean too. Point is: We don't know! And we can't attack them without at least talking to them first. Yes, fighting is necessary sometimes. But we owe it to ourselves to try to settle our differences peacefully first. At least we'd be acting like civilized Xotonians and not a pack of bloodthirsty thyss-cats!"

Sheln hissed. Kalac shook its head.

"Third, and last of all: the Q-sik," said Hudka. "We're supposed to guard the Q-sik, not use it! Most have forgotten, but we tried using it once before, and that brought disaster upon our people."

Everyone knew that Great Jalasu Jhuk had tasked us with protecting the Q-sik. That was its first commandment. I didn't understand what Hudka meant when it said we'd already used the weapon, but I saw some of the older Xotonians nod knowingly.

"The Q-sik is a weapon so powerful, the legends say it can tear a hole in the very fabric of the universe!" continued Hudka. "That's not something I take lightly. So I'll say it again, loud enough for even old Gatas to hear: We shouldn't use it on the humans!

"Our enemy isn't a pack of humans who can barely shuttle between their home planet and this little asteroid. The real enemy is out there. Watching. Waiting for us to do something stupid."

"Oh, please," said Sheln, "you can't seriously mean—"

"The Vorem," said Hudka ominously.

CHAPTER THREE

The crowd exploded at the mention of the Vorem. Most were laughing, although I thought I could hear a nervous pitch in it.

Every Xotonian youngling was told frightening tales of the evil Vorem Dominion, an ancient empire that supposedly ruled the stars and all the black spaces between. In our legends, the Vorem had chased Jalasu Jhuk all over the galaxy. Our Great Progenitor always used its wits and courage to stay one step ahead of them.

If you didn't finish your chores, the elders chided us, a Vorem centurion might just come and get you. If you misbehaved, the Vorem imperator would leave you a lump of black tourmaline instead of a present for the Feast of Zhavend.

Past a certain age, few truly believed these stories. But it was hard to completely shed the fear they inspired.

"Order! Order, please!" cried Loghoz over the ruckus. "Order while the Conclave is in session!"

"Go on. Waste our time," cried Sheln to Hudka, "and by the end of this Conclave, we'll all be your age." By Sheln standards, the joke was a pretty decent one.

"If you were my age, I'd knock your ish'kuts in!" cried Hudka. Sheln lunged forward, and Dyves strained to hold it back.

"Hudka! We all know about the Vorem," said Kalac. "But we can't worry about old stories when we have a real threat, right here on the surface of our asteroid."

"They're not stories," said Hudka. "The Vorem are real. And they still want to destroy us!"

"Hudka, the Observers search the skies continually with their telescopes and scanners," sneered Dyves. "If the Vorem actually existed—if there were any Vorem nearby, we would have seen them."

"No!" cried Hudka. "They don't have to be nearby. Their ships can travel faster than the speed of light. Just like we used to be able to do! That means they can cross an entire galaxy in a matter of hours."

My grand-originator may have had the crowd earlier, but now, faster than the speed of light, Hudka was veering into nutty old coot territory. What it was saying sounded ridiculous, even to me.

"And for your information," said Hudka, "when I was a kid, I did see a Vorem battle cruiser! Saw it. Plain as the sun, blinking right there on a scanner screen in the Observatory. It was searching this sector, I tell you. Looking for us!"

I doubted that a single one of the assembled Xotonians had not already heard this story. Almost all of them had discounted it as pure nonsense. The crowd started to chatter loudly now, in a tone that was less than respectful. My grand-originator had lost them.

"When you were a kid, T'utzuxe had running water!" someone cried out to much laughter.

"When Hudka was a kid," yelled another, "the sun hadn't formed yet!" An even bigger laugh.

It was one thing for me to tease my own grand-originator about its age. It was quite another for a mob of strangers to do it. I was furious but powerless to do anything.

"Hey, when Hudka was a kid," said Sheln, never content to let a joke die a quiet, dignified death, "it was so long ago that everyone, uh, wore rocks instead of clothes!"

The crowd was silent.

"Because . . . Hudka . . . very old . . ." Sheln trailed off.

"Let the record show," said Loghoz, "there was never any official confirmation of the incident that Hudka describes. Hudka was the only one who actually saw this sup-posed Vorem battle cruiser."

"I take it back, Loghoz," said Hudka. "You are as dumb as you look."

"Hudka, I have had just about enough of your disre-spect!" cried Loghoz, bursting into tears once more. "The Custodian of the Council is an honored and ancient title! For thousands of years, the most punctual and literal-minded member of the Council has held . . ."

Loghoz lectured on, but Hudka was no longer paying attention. "I can see which way this Conclave is headed, kid. Don't need to watch it play out," it said quietly to me. "See you back at home. I'll make us some dinner."

"But Hudka, wait—"

Too late. It had already hobbled off, disappearing into the crowd.

"Thank you, Loghoz. Highly informative," said Kalac, gently cutting off Loghoz's blubbery diatribe midway through a biography of Enuz the Rigid, the third to hold the title of Custodian. "If no one else wishes to make any more motions, I suggest we bring both of the Council's proposals to a vote."

"Wait, wait," said Sheln. "Hudka is so old . . . wait . . . Hudka was a kid so long ago . . . but . . . hold on . . ."

"Oh, give it a rest, Sheln," said Kalac.

The Council called a vote on the two proposals about how our race would deal with the humans: a direct attack or an artificial asteroid-quake. A Grand Conclave is only called to decide matters of great importance, and everyone, young and old, may vote.

The Xotonian people chose the asteroid-quake plan by a vote of 4,217 to 1,871. As far as I could see, there was only one abstention. For some reason, I couldn't bring myself to choose either option.

CHAPTER FOUR

The meeting broke up, and the assembled Xotonians drifted back toward their separate lives. They were still filled with the excitement of a Grand Conclave in which great matters were decided, but now they faced the prospect of going home and making dinner.

I walked across the plaza toward our dwelling, vaguely worrying whether I'd hid the human holographic device well enough, vaguely worrying about the asteroid-quake. Up close, the statue of Jalasu Jhuk looked no less inscrutable.

"Chork-a-zoid!"

"Linod-tron!" I called back on instinct. There came my friend Linod, bounding through the crowd toward me. Linod was small and awkward, with spindly thol'grazes and nervous, bulging eyes.

We had a lot in common. Both of us were shy. Both of

us tended toward daydreaming and obsessing. Both of us hated playing oog-ball. Linod was like an even weirder version of myself, and I therefore felt strongly protective of it.

"Chorkle, you've got to check out this slime mold!" Linod held out a thol'graz dripping with bright purple ooze. "What do you think? And be honest."

"Wow, that's uh . . ." I said. "Wait. Why did you bring a slime mold to the Grand Conclave?" I asked.

"Dunno. Figured I'd teach it about the democratic process. What'd you do today?"

"Me? Oh, nothing. Just went on a special reconnaissance mission. Saw some humans. That's all. No big deal."

"Seriously?" cried Linod. "You have to tell me: Did they have any cool molds or yeasts from their own mysterious planet?"

"What? No," I said. "They had personal rockets!"

"Yeah, right," said Zenyk. The voice came from behind me, but I recognized it instantly. Linod now looked terrified, trying in vain to conceal the purple ooze behind its back.

I turned to face Zenyk: big, dumb, and, of course, Sheln's offspring. Four lackeys stood behind it: Chrow, Skubb, Slal, and Polth.

The crowd had mostly thinned now. We stood alone in a deserted corner of the plaza.

"Say, Chorkle, isn't Hudka your grand-originator?" asked Zenyk, already knowing the answer to the question.

"Why, yes, Zenyk, so Hudka is. I had no idea you were interested in genealogy," I said. "I'm very excited to learn about all your hobbies!"

"You say the hoo-mins have 'personal rockets'? I guess Hudka passed the lying gene down to you, huh?" Zenyk turned to its minions. They laughed on command.

"Wow. And you seem to have inherited Sheln's crowd-pleasing sense of humor, yourself," I said.

"Don't you talk about my originator!" it said, cracking the fribs on all four of its thick thol'grazes. Zenyk was just looking for any excuse.

"Look, you're a bully, and I'm smaller than you," I said. "So why don't you just flatten me and get it over with? It'd be a real time-saver." Linod gaped at me as if to say, *What in the name of Morool are you thinking*?

But the direct approach seemed to throw Zenyk off its game. "Don't you tell me what to do!" it said at last. Admittedly, throwing Zenyk off its game wasn't the hardest thing to do.

"Fine. Don't flatten me," I said, shrugging. "In that case,

I've really got to go. It's been fun, though. We should do this more often."

"Wait. Give me that slime mold," said Zenyk. Linod sank. Partly, I was sure, because it wanted to add the mold to its highly disorganized collection of "fascinating fungi." And partly because it had briefly seemed like we might escape this situation without a pummeling. Linod held out the mold weakly.

"Now why would you want a slime mold?" I asked. "Are you hoping it can tutor you in math?"

Zenyk pulled back to flatten me. Instinctively, I folded in on myself to limit the damage. But the blow never landed.

"That's enough!" said Kalac. Zenyk and I turned. Zenyk put its thol'graz down.

My originator stood glaring at me. Not glaring at the dimwitted brute about to pound its own offspring, but at me!

"We have plenty of trouble with the humans," said Kalac. "But now Xotonian is fighting Xotonian? Unacceptable. You should all know better."

"Sorry, Respected One," said Zenyk, slipping into what it considered a fawning, elder-pleasing tone of voice. "We were just roughhousing. Like good friends do."

Yeah. Zenyk roughhousing my face.

"Don't worry. It's fine," I said. I was torn. Part of me

was happy to be rescued from a Zenyk beating. The bigger part of me felt ashamed that my originator had intervened.

"Go home, Zenyk. You too, Linod," said Kalac. It didn't mention the others by name. They were just extensions of Zenyk. "All of your originators will hear about this."

I was sure that Sheln would be very angry with Zenyk. Angry that Zenyk hadn't even gotten to hit me once.

"Bye, Chorkle," said Linod as it darted off. It was probably terrified of being caught again—this time alone—by Zenyk and friends.

"Bye, Chorkle, old buddy," said Zenyk, cuffing me a little too hard on the back and slowly sauntering off toward its own dwelling. Chrow, Skubb, Slal, and Polth followed a few paces behind, affecting the same exact saunter.

I was alone in the plaza with Kalac. In some ways, I found that more frightening than any bully.

"Honestly, Chorkle," said Kalac. "You disappoint me. A Grand Conclave is no place for fighting. And especially with the progeny of my main opponent on the Council. What your grand-originator did was bad enough. I don't need you compounding my troubles as well."

"I didn't start it," I said. But I knew it was hopeless. There are certain situations—no matter how clear to the younglings involved—that elders simply cannot understand.

"If Zenyk is threatening you, pop it once right in the gul'orp," said Kalac as we walked through the streets of Core-of-Rock toward our dwelling. "Xotonians like Zenyk are cowards. The moment they encounter any resistance, they give up."

"So . . . am I supposed to fight it or not?" I asked, a little annoyed. I doubted if my originator had ever even been in the same situation. As far as I knew, Kalac had always been strong and popular. Not likely to have been troubled by the Zenyks of its own youth.

"There's a time for fighting and a time for peace. You're supposed to use common sense," said Kalac. "You convinced me you had some when I agreed to let you inspect Jehe Canyon. So did you learn anything useful?"

"The humans have rockets!" I said.

"Yes, Chorkle, that's how they got here," said Kalac, sighing.

"No, I mean small rockets. That they ride around on for fun. They were flying all over the place, and one of them kept crashing, and then two of them raced each other and—"

"Chorkle," said Kalac, its voice suddenly grave, "did you see actual humans on the surface?"

"I . . . yes."

"And you watched them? For an extended period of time? Did they see you?"

"No, they didn't! I stayed hidden."

"Are you absolutely sure? Tell the truth."

"Yes, I'm sure," I said. "They didn't see me."

Kalac shook its head. "Chorkle, you promised that you would come home immediately at the first sign of any humans! You aren't a scout. You're just a youngling. If they had seen you, it would have ruined everything, destroyed all our plans. This situation is serious, you know. The time for daydreaming is over." It was a different version of the same speech Kalac always gave me.

"Sorry," I said quietly.

"It's my fault," said Kalac. "I shouldn't have let you go. You just aren't ready for such responsibility." We walked a while in silence.

"There were four of them," I said at last. "I think maybe they were younglings. Like me."

It was several seconds before Kalac responded, "I wasn't aware that the humans had brought any offspring with them."

We had reached the entrance to our dwelling. From the smell wafting out the window, Hudka had already started dinner: mushroom and usk-lizard tail stew.

"When we set off the asteroid-quake," I ventured, "will they get hurt?"

Kalac didn't answer.

"Wash up," it said. "It's time to eat."

CHAPTER FIVE

The days after the Conclave passed slowly for me. I couldn't stop thinking about the four juvenile humans. I spent much of my time (when I wasn't enduring instruction, at least) in the caverns near the exit to the surface. There I sat, listening in on the Nyrt-Snooper, for hours at a time. I had started borrowing the tiny device without permission. So far no one had noticed.

Teams of Xotonians still continued to monitor all the human ship-to-satellite transmissions—despite still not understanding human language—from the Observatory inside Dynusk's Column. But after we had collectively decided on the asteroid-quake as the solution to the human problem, our scouts no longer took the Nyrt-Snoopers out to eavesdrop on their interpersonal radio communications. Maybe listening to them chatter away to one another

Xotonian-ized the enemy too much?

I, on the other hand, couldn't get enough. I always tuned in to the channels where I'd heard the young humans communicate before. Mostly I heard static. Sometimes I listened in on what seemed to be adult human miners using the same frequencies. Once or twice a voice sounded familiar. Was that Crackle-Voice speaking to Lenses? Did I just hear Red-Fur laughing? I could never quite be sure.

As I listened, I would occasionally try to repeat the strange human words I heard. "Gud-moor-ning." "How-ya-doo-un." "O-vur-an-dowt." My gul'orp seemed to be the wrong shape to pronounce them.

Twice, I even sneaked out to Jehe Canyon again. There was never a sign of the young humans, though. It was once again just a boring patch of the boring surface of a boring asteroid.

I spent even more time playing games on the human holographic projector device. When I was absolutely certain I was alone, I would pull it out from under my sleeping-veth and immerse myself in a glowing 3-D world that, as far as I could tell, was in every way superior to reality.

I defended Eo from alien saucers. I raced motorized vehicles before thousands of cheering spectators. I completed fiendish puzzles based upon the correct orientation of

colored blocks. All these shimmering holographic chal-
lenges were a subtle mixture of vexation and pleasure. They
were incredibly addictive.

From the games, more human words began to lodge
themselves in my brain: "Kon-tin-ew." "Eck-struh-life."
"Uh-cheeve-men-tun-loct."

One day, I was playing a game in which a squat human
in red must flatten evil walking mushrooms. Evil walking
mushrooms can be quite a problem in the Unclaimed Tunnels, so I identified very strongly with the theme.

"Guano!" I yelled after losing a life.

"You need a running start to make it over that lava pit,"
said Hudka, nearly scaring me to death. My grand-originator
had apparently been watching me for quite a while. I hadn't
noticed. These hologram games had a strange way of dull-
ing the senses.

"What? I mean—I don't know where I stole this thing
from!" I scrambled to conceal the device. But it was obviously too late for that.

"That's a human computer thingy you've got there, kid,"
said Hudka, shaking its head ominously. "I should really
tell Kalac that you have it. And I will—if you don't let me
play too."

And so my grand-originator was initiated into the secret

cult of the human hologram game. Hudka was pretty good for one so old! Many of the games had two-player modes, and we spent hours competing for the high score in all of them.

Our rivalry was especially fierce in the alien invasion game. Hudka loved blasting those flying saucers right out of the sky. But it could never quite edge me out for the top spot.

During this period, a strange thing began to happen. Between listening to so much human conversation on the Nyrt-Snooper and playing so many human games, my human vocabulary began to grow. Thanks to total cultural immersion and a naturally keen Xotonian memory, I was accidentally beginning to understand their language.

"Xenostryfe III," I said suddenly one day as Hudka and I played the alien-blaster game.

"Did you just sneeze?" asked Hudka.

"No, I—I think that's the name of this hologram game," I said. "You know, the human name." Somehow the letters of the alien alphabet that always displayed at the start of the game suddenly made sense to me. I'd seen them often enough that I'd been able to connect them to specific sounds.

"Xenostryfe III? What in the name of Morool is that supposed to mean?" asked Hudka.

"I'll . . . I'll have to get back to you on that," I said as my life meter dipped to zero under the onslaught of flying saucers. The hologram faded monochrome gray. Game over.

"Learned to read human but forgot how to play," snickered Hudka. "Seriously, get your priorities straight, Chorkle."

But from that moment on, I made a conscious effort to retain and understand all the human words I heard or read. And slowly, little by little, they started to make sense.

Before I knew it, the asteroid-quake mission was only a few days away.

All five members of the Council convened at the Vault, a pyramid-shaped building near Ryzz Plaza constructed entirely from lead.

The Vault was the sort of thing that you saw every day of your life but never really took a good look at. It stood in sharp contrast to the typical Xotonian structures, which are dome-shaped and built from stone blocks. The Vault had no windows and a single door made of solid iridium, with an eight-pointed star inset. This was where Great Jalasu Jhuk had put the Q-sik for safekeeping.

Though the general public was forbidden from attending the opening, I secretly watched from behind the column of a nearby building. I'd changed my skin to the shade of the surrounding architecture. Sometimes Xotonian camouflage works even on Xotonians.

Kalac approached the door, beside which was a numeric keypad. Consulting a yellowing scrap of paper—apparently a relic passed down to each Chief of the Council since ancient times—it pressed a series of digits into the pad. I was close enough that I could see Kalac's brips punch the buttons: 9-1-5-6-7-2-3-4.

There was a pause. Then the door began to slide downward with a scraping rumble.

If Jalasu Jhuk didn't want Xotonians to use the Q-sik, I wondered, why leave instructions for opening the Vault?

But pondering the will of the ancients is a sucker's game. That was an old expression that Hudka probably made up.

The door was open now. A pale, eerie glow shone from inside. From my vantage point, I couldn't quite see the Vault's interior. The Council huddled nervously on the threshold. At last, Kalac stepped through the door.

A few long moments later, my originator came out carrying the source of the light: the Q-sik itself.

It was like nothing I'd ever seen before. The Q-sik appeared to be a glowing tetrahedron that spun slowly inside several concentric rings of tarnished, iridescent metal.

On its base were several complex controls and inputs, which allowed for its use. On top, the Q-sik came to a sharp point from which, I guessed, it would fire its energy beam, a blast powerful enough to destroy several kilometers of solid rock, powerful enough to rip a hole in the universe, if the legends were to be believed. I was surprised to see how small the device was.

From where I stood, I could also see the iridium statue of Jalasu Jhuk in Ryzz Plaza, now reflecting glints of the Q-sik's light. This little thing was what our Great Progenitor was so worried about?

The other Council members shrank back from the Q-sik. Only Kalac looked resolute as it strode past them, holding it aloft. In its other thol'graz, it carried a crumbling manual.

For better or worse, the ancient weapon would now decide the fate of the Xotonian people.

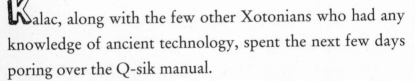

CHAPTER SIX

Kalac, along with the few other Xotonians who had any knowledge of ancient technology, spent the next few days poring over the Q-sik manual.

The heavy tome turned out to be a collection of meticulous notes, written and placed inside the Vault by Great Jalasu Jhuk itself. No one had much time to dwell on this remarkable historical discovery, however. Kalac and the others were too busy trying to understand the workings of the Q-sik enough to fire it.

Now came the day of the asteroid-quake mission. Kalac, Hudka, and I were eating breakfast (rild-sauce over cold svur-noodles) together in our dwelling. Tensions were high. Well, higher than normal.

"Mark my words," said Hudka. "You're making the biggest mistake in Xotonian history. Even bigger than the time we declared it legal to raise giant spiders for food inside city limits!"

"I'm not having this discussion again," said Kalac. "There was a Grand Conclave. I seem to recall that you were there, Hudka. There is no turning back now. We reached a decision as a society."

"A bad decision," said Hudka. As a rule, Hudka never let Kalac, or anybody, have the last word in an argument.

"But what if the humans aren't evil?" I asked, slurping down a gul'orp-ful of svur-noodles. "Maybe we could work with them instead of against them?"

"You've brought this up before, Chorkle," said Kalac wearily. "And I have told you that the stakes are simply too high. I'll admit that I don't know for certain that the humans mean us harm. And I'll grant that there might be a small chance that diplomacy might work. But suppose it didn't. What then?"

"Just because the right thing to do might not work doesn't mean it's not the right thing to do," said Hudka. "And we're supposed to guard the Q-sik. Removing it from the Vault is a mistake."

"Now is not the time!" snapped Kalac. My originator's nerves were running high. In just a few hours, it would be leading the asteroid-quake mission.

"You two give me more trouble than all the humans combined," said Kalac, rising from the table. "I have to go. There are still final preparations to make."

"But there must be something we can do!" I said. "To make sure that the young—that no humans are needlessly hurt in the quake."

Kalac stared at me, surprised. I don't know that I'd ever confronted my originator so directly.

"Chorkle," it said slowly, "the success of this plan is crucial to the very survival of our species. If humans are hurt or, yes, even killed, that is the price that must be paid. Do you understand this?"

I didn't say anything.

"Do you understand, Chorkle?"

"Yes," I mumbled.

"Good," said Kalac. "Now I must go." And my originator walked out the front door of our dwelling. The next time I saw Kalac—at dinnertime, I supposed—the human problem would be solved.

I looked at Hudka. On most days, it would have had the hologram game out the instant Kalac was gone. We both would have been gleefully stomping evil mushrooms or racing motorized vehicles in endless laps in a human city called "In-dee-uh-nap-oh-luss."

Not today, though. My grand-originator sat at the breakfast table, staring at the wall. Hudka looked as small and worried as I'd ever seen it.

"I don't want anyone to get hurt," I said. "I mean, if the human race came up with hologram games, then they can't be all bad, can they?" It was an odd defense of an entire species. Hudka stared at me.

"Nobody is all bad," said Hudka. "Not Xotonians. Not humans."

"I think—I think I should do something."

"Then do what you need to do," said Hudka.

Twenty-seven turns later, I stood at the entrance to the surface.

CHAPTER SEVEN

I walked across the surface of Gelo, running through human phrases in my mind. Red T'utzuxe hung heavy in the sky.

Up ahead, I saw their mothership for the first time. A huge metal globe squatting on the surface of our asteroid. Rusted and pockmarked, bristling with spiny antennae, emblazoned with the flags of many Eo countries. I recognized a few of them from a particular hologram game in which two teams of human males attempted to kick a white ball into the net of their opponents.

A series of smaller pods radiated out from the mothership, each connected back to it via a flexible tube. I guessed this configuration allowed the humans to travel among the various pods, using the mothership as a central hub.

In the distance, big mining machinery sat parked in

silence. If the human workday was over, then at least no one would be underground when the mines collapsed.

Why was I even here? Was I going to warn the humans somehow? Had I come as some sort of self-appointed Xotonian diplomat? Even if the young humans turned out to be friendly, who knew how their adults would behave? What if they took one look at me and decided to shoot me with their primitive—yet still quite lethal—projectile weapons? Standing this close to a bustling hive of them, I felt far from safe.

I checked my chronometer. Still three hours until the asteroid-quake. Then, if Kalac's calculations were correct, the ground here would begin to shake and churn, possibly destroying the human mothership. I didn't want to be here when that happened.

Something crackled over the Nyrt-Snooper. It was a human voice I didn't recognize. It sounded female. I heard it command another human called "Danny" to remove . . . something from their pod, immediately. Then there was a grudging yet affirmative response in a familiar register. It was Crackle-Voice!

So Crackle-Voice was named "Danny." Or at least I thought so. My human language skills were still pretty bad. "Danny" might actually be the human word for "digestive ailment."

I scanned the pods. There was movement inside one of them. The small light outside its airlock changed from red to green. I snuck closer, my skin a perfect Gelo blue-gray.

The pod's airlock slid open with a hiss. It was Danny. He was wearing a spacesuit, and he had two large metal cylinders with him.

He hefted one of the cylinders, walked about a hundred meters away from the spacecraft, and dumped it out on the ground. Its contents seemed mostly to be rotting organic matter. Human garbage.

Did humans really just dump their waste right next to where they lived? Perhaps there was some truth to the Xotonian stereotype that they were a pack of filthy slobs.

Danny replaced the first cylinder and went to empty the second. Something seized me. I still don't know what. But before I thought better of it, I darted into the airlock and climbed up the wall onto the ceiling. I hung there, my skin now the warm beige of the ship's interior.

To one side of the airlock were the four personal rockets I'd seen the humans riding in Jehe Canyon, heaped together in a sort of standing pile.

Danny returned to the airlock. He walked over to a glowing console and punched a button. The outside hatch slowly rolled closed. Once it had formed an airtight seal, the inner door slid open with a whoosh as oxygen-rich human air rushed in. Air, I noticed, that was very similar to that in the Gelo caverns.

Danny took off his spacesuit and stuffed it inside a small metal box—one of several beside the airlock—then ambled off down the hallway. He never once looked up.

There I was, inside a human spacecraft.

I was inside a human spacecraft!

I crept along the ceiling. The pod was warm and cramped. All blinking consoles, tangled wires, and inconvenient angles. It had a central hallway that gave access to six individual chambers. At the far end I saw what appeared to be another airlock, this one attached to one of the tubes that led back toward the mothership.

I waited for Danny to return. He didn't. The pod was empty. I dropped to the floor and touched one of the doors. It quickly slid open with a pleasing hiss. I stepped back. It hissed closed. I stepped forward. It hissed open again.

By Jalasu Jhuk, these humans sure had it figured out! This—this was an achievement on par with the hologram game. Why must Xotonians constantly be forced to open our own doors? I wondered. What drudgery! Imagine the time we'd save over the course of a lifetime if our doors simply had the good sense to open themselves.

I mean, obviously our great ancestors had intended us to have self-opening doors. I remembered the ancient door of the Vault opening of its own accord once the correct combination was put in. Why hadn't we heeded their wisdom?

After making the human door open six or seven more times, I entered the chamber beyond. It was messy, even by human standards. A big overstuffed couch dominated the space. It faced a deactivated tele-visual console on the wall. Behind the couch was a green table marked with white lines and divided in half by a short vertical mesh. On the table were two red paddles and a little white ball. Beside them was a box.

I took a closer look. The box was covered in human language characters. I tried to read them, but I could only make out the human word for "ice." The box bore the picture of a juvenile human male, grinning grotesquely and consuming a bright pink bar of . . . something.

I reached into the box. It was full of bar-shaped things, each covered in a shiny, crinkly protective coating, almost like a tiny human spacesuit. I pulled one out and tore away the coating. Sure enough, a sticky pink bar inside. I sniffed it. Organic, mostly. Not ice, though.

I took a bite. The taste was heavenly. No, beyond heavenly. Sweet. Gummy. Delightfully unnatural! I finished the bar. And another. And one more after that. In fact, I wanted nothing more than to consume the whole box. All the boxes. Were there more boxes anywhere?

Self-opening doors, hologram games, personal rockets, and now these pink bars. In that sugary euphoria, I was ready to admit the cultural superiority of humankind. If there were just six thousand more of these delicious bars—one for every Xotonian—I was sure there could be peace between our two peoples. But secretly, I knew the truth. If there were six thousand more, I would eat all of them.

Just as I was finishing my fifth, I heard footsteps in the hallway. Someone was coming. I replaced the box and looked around for somewhere to hide.

Across the room was a grate at floor level. I slid it aside and hid in the metal air duct behind it.

Four juvenile humans entered the chamber with great noise and commotion. It was Danny and the three others I'd seen before!

Here they were, not three meters away, the whole reason I had come. But just what, exactly, was I going to do? I imagined leaping out from behind the grate.

"Hello, young humans!" I would say in accented but passable human-ese. "I've been secretly observing you, and I just wanted to let you know that my originator is going

65

to cause an asteroid-quake that might kill you and all of your families! I hope we can still be friends." And that was honestly the best I could come up with. So what I actually did was stay hidden and keep my gul'orp shut.

All four plopped down onto the couch. Red-Fur jostled for space at the end. From their conversation, I deduced that his human name was "Little Gus."

And, strangely, they referred to Danny as "Hollins" instead. Perhaps "Danny" was merely a title. Like "Custodian of the Council" or "Master of Nyshves."

Anyway, Hollins and No-Lenses, whose real name was "Becky," immediately started bickering with one another. Lenses, or "Nicki," intervened and helped them to make peace. I got the sense that Hollins had ultimately won this round.

Hollins remotely activated the tele-visual console. The screen lit up. What were they about to watch? A transmission from their leader, perhaps? Some important scientific or moral lesson to be imparted upon them?

What followed was a ninety-minute broadcast of fist-fights, shootouts, and fiery explosions, only interrupted by brief, unrelated transmissions that showcased human consumer goods.

The children watched as one adult male—who called

himself a "homicide detective"—embarked upon a bloody quest for vengeance against those responsible for the death of his partner. In practice, this meant shooting half the people in the city. The young humans laughed and applauded at the bloodiest moments of on-screen carnage.

By the end of the broadcast, I was horrified. Maybe these aliens weren't like me at all. Maybe Sheln was right. Maybe they were bloodthirsty. Evil.

Oog-ball is a brutal sport that many Xotonians love. But even the most ardent oog-ball fan wouldn't want to see an hour and a half of murder!

An hour and a half. The asteroid-quake! I looked at my chronometer. Only thirty minutes left until the asteroid-quake! Then the very ground beneath the mothership could collapse. I had to get out of here, and fast.

I had come to warn these humans. Only now I was even more terrified that if I revealed myself, they would all pull out guns, like the man on the screen, and riddle me with bloody holes! But even if I'd wanted to leave without warning them, they were blocking my only exit.

So I panicked and I did the only thing I could think of: I discharged my stink-gland.

CHAPTER EIGHT

Yes, we Xotonians have a stink-gland. Just like our camouflage, at some point in the distant past it must have evolved as a natural defense mechanism against predators. These days we mostly use it to clear out parties that have gone on too long.

I only discharged a little. At first, I worried that humans lacked the olfactory sensitivity to notice. If the condition of their footwear—the rubbery coverings that all four had kicked off upon entering the room—was any indication, they had a much weaker sense of smell than Xotonians.

But soon the odor wafted toward them. First Little Gus crinkled his nose. Then they all began to retch and gag and cover their faces and shout. They pointed at one another in accusation.

But my plan worked. They all cleared out of the room,

each believing one of the others responsible for the stench.

Now was my chance. Quietly, I slid the grate from the wall and crept out into the empty, darkened chamber. As I made my way toward the exit, something caught my third and fourth eyes.

The box of sticky-sweet bars was right where I had left it. Surely I had time for just one more. This might be my last chance ever. . . .

I plunged my thol'graz into the box and pulled out a bar. I quickly unwrapped it—by now I was an expert at un-wrapping them—and took another sublime bite. Outside, I heard someone coming.

I managed to scramble back into the vent and replace the grate just in time.

It was Hollins. He'd tied a red cloth over his nose to block the smell. He plopped back down on the couch and continued to watch the screen.

Becky followed him, aggressively spraying some sort of cloyingly sweet gas from a pink metal canister—an artificial counter-stink. To me, it smelled even worse than anything I had secreted. But Becky evidently found it preferable.

Next Nicki entered carrying a small motorized fan that she kept pointed right at her face. She went to the wall and fiddled with a console. A strong gust of air blew from the vent behind me. She had adjusted the pod's life-support system to increase ventilation.

Finally, Little Gus came bounding back in. He was now wearing the transparent helmet of his spacesuit over his normal clothes and breathing his own air supply. He settled on the couch beside the others.

The humans had effectively stink-proofed the room. So much for my not-so-brilliant plan. I needed another option.

Perhaps I could follow the ventilation system to a different grate and exit from there? I turned and headed deeper into the duct. The airflow grew stronger with each meter I walked. Soon, I came to a massive spinning fan blade covered in a sturdy metal grate. It completely blocked my path. I turned back.

Only ten minutes left until the quake. Why hadn't I left when I had the chance? Why had I even come here in the first place?

I watched the screen helplessly from behind the grate. Now it showed a completely different scenario: A human male and female bickered over the preparation of an elaborate feast. Every few seconds there was a loud burst of ghostly, disembodied laughter (that neither the man nor the woman seemed to notice!). Somehow this was even more disturbing than the previous broadcast.

Just then, there was another one of the short interrupting

transmissions. New footage, at an increased sound volume, showed several grinning juvenile humans running around and playing outside on Eo. They laughed in a strange, artificial way. Now they were eating something. It was the sweet pink bars! One of the on-screen children held up the box and said, "Feeney's Original Astronaut Ice Cream."

That was why I hadn't exited the craft: those accursed, delicious pink bars. They had entranced me with their sugary magic. While the pod was empty, I'd wasted several seconds trying to get another sweet, sweet fix. I shook my head ruefully at the box, still clutched in my thol'graz.

"Curse you, Feeney's Original Astronaut Ice Cream," I said under my breath.

Wait. I was still holding the box. Why was I still holding the box? In my panic, I had accidentally brought it with me into the grate! On a day full of mistakes and miscalculations, this was my greatest.

Now the juveniles were up from the couch. They were looking for something. Of course they were. The console had reminded them that they had a box of Feeney's Original Astronaut Ice Cream bars lying around in the pod somewhere. Why wouldn't they want to eat them?

They searched under furniture, behind electronic equipment, on top of shelves. Nicki held up a shiny discarded wrapper. Hollins held up another. I'd left a trail right back to my hiding place.

Kalac often said that I lacked common sense. At that moment, it would have been hard to argue.

Becky picked up the last wrapper, right outside the vent. I was frozen in terror. I dared not move for fear of making a sound.

She turned to look at the others; then she pulled the vent aside. The humans found me hiding inside their ventilation system. All four stared in silence, mouths hanging open.

First contact. Two intelligent species, human and Xotonian, meeting one another in the infinite void of the cosmos, against all odds. If the circumstances had been different, I might have commemorated this historic occasion in some way. A moving speech, say, or maybe just a simple gesture of peace between our two peoples.

Instead, I discharged my stink gland. And this time I discharged all the stink I had left, right in Becky's face.

As she shrieked and tumbled backward, I somersaulted over her.

"Stop!" cried Hollins, and he dove at me. I sprang high into the air, and he crashed into the green table, taking it down.

At the height of my jump, I grabbed onto a light fixture on the ceiling and clung there.

Little Gus took a running go off the couch and leaped, straining to reach me. But his jump wasn't quite high enough. Or maybe he just wasn't tall enough. Either way, he crash-landed right on top of Hollins, who had just managed to get back on his feet. Somewhere Becky was still screaming.

Just as I'd feared, the second they'd seen me, these humans wanted to kill me!

I dropped to the floor and ran hard for the door. My path was clear now. I was going to make it.

At the last possible instant, Nicki reached in from the side and slammed her fist on a button beside the door. As I hurtled toward it, I never heard the expected hiss of automatic opening. She had locked it.

I slammed hard into the door, face first, and slowly slid down to the floor.

As I lay there, losing consciousness, a strange jolt ran through me. For a single instant, I felt that an energy of unimaginable power had just been unleashed . . . somewhere nearby. It crackled on my skin and flowed through my body and even into the spaces between my molecules.

The next instant it was gone, and the whole world began to shake.

All was black.

CHAPTER NINE

I awoke with a powerful face-ache. My bones were still rattling. Or maybe everything but my bones was rattling?

I blinked. Four human faces blinked back at me. They were talking to each other in hushed and fearful tones.

I shrieked in panic, and they all jumped back. I struggled hard, but something held me fast. While I was unconscious, the humans had apparently tied me up with some sort of strong plastic rope.

What were they going to do? Torture me? Kill me? Eat me?

Hollins was talking to me now. He was saying something in human about "alien" and "prisoner" and "no escape." I strained to understand. He brandished one of the rubbery red paddles from the green table and tried to keep his voice steady.

My thoughts were still fuzzy. Everything around me seemed to be shaking. Loose objects were skittering around the room and falling from shelves. Even the human children seemed to struggle to stay on their feet.

That's when it dawned on me: the asteroid-quake had already begun. Somewhere, under the surface, Kalac and the others had fired the Q-sik. They had vaporized the solid rock that supported the ground beneath us. Now caverns and tunnels below were collapsing.

"Us need go," I said in words that I thought were human, in a tone that I thought was reassuring. Apparently not. All the humans jumped back again. Hearing me try to speak their language seemed to terrify them even more than me screaming.

"Asteroid-quake," I said, again in human. Was "asteroid-quake" even a word in their language?

Then a new voice came from . . . nowhere. It was loud and female. It carried no inflection, so it was easier for me to follow. "Warning. Hazardous seismic event detected. Moderate damage to outer hull has occurred," it said. "Automatic takeoff procedures initiated."

The starship's sensors had realized that the asteroid-quake was happening. This had triggered some sort of pre-programmed launch sequence that would carry the ship to the safety of space.

Good, I thought, that means the humans won't be hurt.

They'll be in space before the ship is crushed or swallowed by the ground. It took my addled brain another half second to realize that I would be going to space with them.

"Please. Chorkle go. Chorkle go," I pleaded in human. Nicki stared at me. After a moment, she made a slow move toward me. Hollins stopped her. The humans all looked as confused and afraid as I was. Apparently they'd never been through "automated takeoff procedures" before either.

In addition to the asteroid-quake, I now felt the mechanical rumblings of the ship preparing for launch. Its inner workings began to churn and shift behind the walls. Out the viewports, the scenery of Gelo began to slide sideways. The whole pod was now rolling, further inhibiting anyone's ability to stand upright. Little Gus fell backward onto the box of Feeney's Original Astronaut Ice Cream.

I guessed that the mothership was retracting all her pods inward—and collapsing their connecting flexible tubes—before she blasted off.

Becky ran out the door of the room. She returned shortly. I gathered from her rapid report that the pod's access to the mothership had been restricted for takeoff.

"Please take your seats," said the always calm voice of the ship. "Make sure your seat belts are securely fastened low and tight around your waist."

Just then the tele-visual screen blinked to life. It was an adult male and female, huddled into the frame.

The young humans crowded in front of the screen, and everyone began talking at once. The adults looked frightened, but they were telling the young humans not to worry. Everything was going to be okay.

The young humans kept interrupting. They were trying to tell the adults that there was an alien—seriously, a real, live alien—inside the pod. Were they talking about me?

The adults were confused. At last Hollins physically rotated the screen so that it pointed right at me. A new shade of terror spread across the adults' faces as they saw me. I wriggled uncomfortably on the floor.

Then the tele-visual screen flickered. It was now showing a video about procedures in the event of a crash; oddly placid people folded their heads toward their knees. Nicki punched the remote frantically. Becky banged on the side of the screen. It was no use—they couldn't get it back to the adults.

"Launch sequence in twenty-nine . . . twenty-eight . . . twenty-seven . . ." the computer voice said. Outside, I could see the surface of the asteroid roiling and shaking like water in the quake.

"Chorkle go," I said faintly.

The juvenile humans looked at one another. At last, they all sat down on seats that folded out of the wall. They securely fastened their seat belts.

"Five . . . four . . . three . . . two . . ."

There was a blinding light and a sound like a hundred stars exploding at once. I felt myself getting heavier, crushed into the metal floor of the chamber by some invisible force. It was hard to breathe. It was even harder to think.

I turned to look at the humans. All their eyes were closed tight, and their skin sagged. Tears streamed down Little Gus's face. Outside, the surface of the asteroid fell away in a cloud of fire.

"Warning! Warning! Class G foreign organic matter detected in pod sixteen," said the ship's computer. Her voice was barely audible over the launch. "Quarantine protocol executed. Pod sixteen . . . ejected."

There was a new sound now, a loud pressurized rip. Suddenly I wasn't heavy anymore. In fact, I weighed nothing at all.

For a few beautiful moments, I floated weightlessly through the air. A pristinely wrapped bar of Feeney's Original Astronaut Ice Cream slowly twirled past my face, a fellow traveler on the same fantastic voyage. I tried to grab it, but I was apparently tied up. When had that happened?

Through the viewport outside, I saw the human mothership shrinking away into space. She was trailing fire like a comet. Goodbye, human mothership!

The surface of Gelo was growing now. Familiar craters and canyons were rushing right toward the pod. Hello, asteroid!

"Brace for impact," said the ship's computer. Wow, I completely understood that, I thought. My human language skills certainly were improving.

And then I smashed hard into the wall, which for some reason was also the ground.

So that's why you need a seat belt, I thought.

And for the second time that day, I lost consciousness.

CHAPTER TEN

I awoke to the sound of sobbing.

It was dark, and I couldn't move. This time it wasn't just a face-ache. I had a pretty good everything-ache going.

"Help," said someone above me.

The lights flickered on, and I could see clearly. The room was on its side. I was half buried in a heap of loose objects against one wall. My face was pressed against a round viewport. Outside it, all I could see was Gelo dirt.

The whole pod, I realized, was lying on its side. I tried to get up, but I couldn't. I was still bound as tightly as ever.

Hollins and Becky were helping Nicki out of her seat on what was now the floor. Or maybe it was Hollins and Nicki helping Becky out of the seat. I couldn't tell. In the crash, Nicki must have lost her vision lenses. Now the duplicates were eerily interchangeable.

I realized where the crying was coming from. On the far wall—now the ceiling of the sideways room—hung Little Gus. He was still tightly strapped into his foldout chair, and every tuft of his red hair was standing on end. He looked terrified.

"I'm gonna get you down," said Hollins. He jumped straight up as high as he could. But he was nowhere close to reaching Little Gus.

"Can help," I said in human, startling them all.

"Help? We don't need your help!" cried Hollins, suddenly remembering that I existed. "You caused all this!"

"No cause," I said. "Not want."

"Yes cause!" said Hollins. "You're the 'class G foreign organic material' that the computer detected. That's why the ship dumped us back on the asteroid. We should be up there with our parents." He pointed to the spot where the viewport should have been, but that was now actually the floor.

"Bad computer," I said.

"Our computers are just fine!" said Hollins. "Don't you talk about our computers, Martian." He was shaking with anger.

"Hollins, I can't believe you're losing an argument with an alien," cried Becky. I could tell it was Becky because her duplicate had thankfully recovered her lenses.

"You can't reason with it," she said. "It wants to rip

your face off and lay its eggs in your lungs. We have to—to kill it!"

"No, we can't lose our heads. We need to assess the situation calmly," said Hollins. He sounded pretty far from calm.

"I'm sorry, but that thing sprayed me with poison!" Becky was still strongly redolent of Xotonian stink and not happy about it.

"We don't know it was poison," said Nicki. "It could have just been waste."

"Great. Thank you, Nicki," said Becky. "Yes, it could have been waste. That makes me feel so much better."

"I mean, the stuff it sprayed at you smelled bad, right?" said Nicki. "What? Just thinking out loud, here."

"Hey! I'm still stuck on the ceiling!" moaned Little Gus.

"Can help," I said. "Can help Gus."

"Oh God," said Becky, burying her head in her hands. "It knows our names. How does it know our names?"

"Just keep quiet, Martian," said Hollins. He rummaged around in the heap on the floor until he found the red paddle. Then he pointed it at me.

"Where are our parents? Are they coming back?" whined Little Gus.

"Pod impact assessment," said the ship's computer voice. "Warning. Critical damage to communications and life-support systems detected. Oxygen leaks in tanks three, four, five, seven, nine, and ten."

"What?" said Becky.

"Three hours thirty-one minutes of oxygen remaining," said the computer. "Please commence emergency evacuation." All the humans moaned in unison. Little Gus was crying again now.

"The pod must have gotten damaged in the crash," said Nicki.

"Okay. Okay," said Hollins. "First we get Little Gus down. Gus, can you unfasten your seat belt?"

"It's stuck," said Gus pitifully as he tried to disengage the metal buckle.

In frustration, Hollins again tried to jump toward the ceiling. Again he was at least a meter short.

"Maybe you two could lift me up to him?" said Nicki.

Hollins and Becky each hoisted one of Nicki's feet and pushed her up toward the ceiling. She stretched to her full length, but her fingertips were still a few dozen centimeters short. She strained even further and upset the balance of the three-person pyramid. Becky wobbled, and they all fell into a heap.

"It's okay, Little Gus," said Hollins as he sat on the floor, panting. Gus wailed.

"Can help Gus," I said. "Can climb."

All four of them turned and stared at me.

"I don't know . . . maybe we should let it try," said Nicki at last.

"If we set that thing free," said Becky, "this whole thing ends with face-huggers flying out of our stomachs! You know that, right?" ·

"Please," said Little Gus. "I have to pee."

"Martian. Alien. Whatever you are," said Hollins, "if I let you go, you have to swear that you won't try to escape."

"Great. The honor system," said Becky. "The honor system will save us all."

"Do you swear? On your mother's life?" said Hollins, and he stared right into my eyes.

"Mother . . . not have," I said. I wasn't articulate enough to explain what an originator was.

"Oh, come on!" cried Becky. "It's just pretending to be an orphan for sympathy!"

"Do you swear on—on something really important?" said Hollins.

"Yes," I said. "Swear. On Jalasu Jhuk."

"Three hours twenty minutes of oxygen remaining," said the computer voice.

Hollins sighed. Then he crouched down beside me and

untied my ropes. I flexed my thol'grazes a bit. It was a relief to be free.

I stood up. Hollins, Becky, and Nicki all jumped back. The way they were acting, you'd think I was a feral thyss-cat, not a terrified young Xotonian in way over its head.

"One false move, and I'm making alien soup," said Becky, hoisting a broken chair leg above her head for use as a bludgeoning weapon.

"Coming," I said to Little Gus, trying to reassure him.

"Hold on a second, guys," said Little Gus. "Maybe I don't have to pee that bad."

But it was too late. I had already leaped up to the ceiling and was clinging there upside down. We Xotonians are excellent climbers, capable of finding a grip on most surfaces. It's necessary when you spend 90 percent of your life trying to get around in slippery caves.

Slowly I crept across the ceiling toward Little Gus's seat. He leaned as far away from me as possible.

"You know what, I think I'm fine here, actually," he said. "Maybe just toss me up a magazine to pass the time or something."

Gingerly, I put my thol'graz on his arm. He flinched.

"Please don't eat my face," he whimpered quietly. Still clinging to the ceiling with my fel'grazes, I began to fiddle with the snap. Little Gus was right. It was stuck tight.

"Need cut," I said.

Hollins sighed, then pulled a metal object from his pocket. He unfolded it to show me what it was: a small knife.

"Seriously? Now you're giving the alien a stabbing weapon?" cried Becky. "Hey, maybe it needs a machete and a couple of grenades too."

"Odds are that its species already has way more advanced weapons than us anyway," said Nicki. "A knife isn't going to matter."

"You really know how to set my mind at ease, sis," said Becky. "I think it's that special bond that only twins share."

Nicki shrugged, "Thinking out loud."

Hollins refolded the knife and tossed it up to me. I caught it and went to work sawing through Little Gus's strap.

It was slow going, but at last I heard a pop. Little Gus swung free from the seat and dangled from my thol'graz. Becky and Hollins strained to reach his feet and lower him safely to the floor.

"I'll be back in a second!" said Little Gus and he scrambled through the chamber's sideways door into the sideways hallway beyond.

Hollins, Becky, and Nicki looked up at me. I was on the ceiling, out of their reach. And now I had a weapon. I turned the blade over in my thol'graz. It would keep them back. Maybe just long enough for me to escape?

I dropped to the ground and handed back the knife.

"Thank you," said Nicki.

"Thanks," mumbled Hollins.

"You're still our prisoner," said Becky. "And you're not luring me into a false sense of security."

"Whew. That's much better," said Little Gus as he returned through the sideways door. "Bathroom's crazy though. Everything's sideways. I, er, wouldn't go in there—"

Just then the tele-visual screen flicked on. It was the male and female adult humans from before. The video was staticky, often freezing for moments at a time.

"Danny? Kids?" said the female adult. Both of the adults were crying.

"Mom! Dad!" cried Hollins, leaping over debris to get closer to the now sideways screen. "Can you hear me, Mom?"

"Commander Hollins! Mr. Hollins!" said Becky to the screen. Apparently both of these adults were called Hollins too. Perhaps most humans were named Hollins?

Becky continued, "Commander, do you know if our parents—"

"Kids, if you can hear us," said Commander Hollins,

"please don't panic. We're fine here. If there really is an—an alien life form there with you, do not approach it. Leave it alone. If you can, lock yourselves in a different room within the pod." She was trembling. The pain and fear in her voice were obvious, even to a member of another species.

"Mom!" cried Danny Hollins. But the woman on the screen couldn't hear him. The transmission was one-way.

"Nicole, Rebecca, your mom and dad are fine. Augustus, your father is fine too," said the adult male Hollins. "We've already been in contact with—with some military people, scientists. They're analyzing the footage from your transmission. They're trying to figure out what that creature—what it is we're up against."

"See," said Becky, "it's a war."

"Our ship was seriously damaged during that quake," said the female Hollins, apparently Commander. "We must make some repairs and refuel before we'll be able to land on the asteroid again. Our engineers are saying it will take at least six days. If there was any way we could come back for you right now, we would."

"Six days?" said Little Gus in disbelief.

"In the meantime," said Mr. Hollins, choking up. "In the meantime, the asteroid's orbit is going to put it on the other side of Mars. That means no radio contact for a while.

Before that happens, if there's any way you can send a message to let us know what's going on—if we just knew you
were okay—"

He couldn't continue. He was overcome with emotion.

"Don't worry, children. We're coming back with a rescue team, with soldiers," said Commander Hollins. "Just
stay safe for six days. We'll—"

And then the screen went black, and she was gone.

"Three hours of oxygen remaining," said the computer.

CHAPTER ELEVEN

"**W**e need a plan," said Hollins.

I had voluntarily allowed them to retie me. Although this time I noticed that Hollins didn't tie my bonds quite as tightly.

"Okay, first off, we have more than three hours," said Nicki, "because we have spacesuits with their own oxygen tanks. That means each of us has at least ten additional hours of air before it runs out."

"Thirteen hours total," said Hollins. "Still not even close to six days."

"Really? And they say Nicki's the genius," said Becky, her voice sarcastic.

"Becky, if you're not going to help, then why don't you just be quiet?" growled Hollins.

"Seriously? Why am I the only one who's worried

about the alien in the corner that wants to murder us?" she screamed, pointing at me.

"Murder?" I said.

"See? See! It said 'murder'!" cried Becky. But no one really seemed to be paying attention to her.

"Is there any way to fix the pod's oxygen tanks?" asked Hollins.

"I think we'd need a welding torch and something to patch it with," said Nicki. "Stuff we don't have."

"I can't get this thing to work either," said Little Gus. He'd been fiddling with the tele-visual console for a few minutes. "It won't send an outgoing transmission."

"The computer said that the communications system was damaged," said Hollins. "I guess that's what it meant: no way to radio out."

"Our spacesuit helmets have radios, right?" said Little Gus.

"Not strong enough," said Nicki. "But maybe we could send a message a different way?"

"So we can't call our parents, and we're running out of air," said Hollins.

"Couldn't we just use our rocket-bikes?" asked Little Gus. "And fly up to the ship?" I gathered "rocket-bikes" is what the humans called the personal rockets stored in the airlock.

"Nope," said Hollins. "The bikes don't have enough

power to escape the asteroid's gravity. Or any life-support systems. Even if they did, our parents are probably already thousands of kilometers away by now. Rocket-bikes just aren't meant for space travel."

Gus sank.

"So much for being the first kids in a semipermanent asteroid-mining colony," said Becky. "Awesome idea, Mom and Dad. Parents of the Year."

"Come on, Becky. You liked having your picture on the news at the time," said Nicki.

"Yeah, but this was supposed to be a year of skipping seventh grade, a bunch of parades back on Earth, and one heck of a college entrance essay. Now we're going to die with the whole world watching."

"We're going to die?" asked Little Gus.

"No," said Hollins. "Nobody's going to die. We'll figure something out."

"What's the point?" said Becky, slumping down on the couch.

"Becky, in any moment of decision, the best thing you can do is the right thing, the next best thing is the wrong thing, and the worst thing you can do is nothing," said Hollins. "Teddy Roosevelt said that."

"Who?" asked Little Gus.

"The twenty-sixth president of the United States," said Hollins. "He was also an explorer and an author and one of the great—"

"Stop!" cried Becky. "The only thing that could make dying worse is getting a history lesson at the same time!"

"Wait," said Nicki suddenly. "That's it. What you said."

"Teddy Roosevelt?" said Hollins.

"No, sorry. What Becky said! Before!"

"College entrance essay?" said Becky.

"You said the whole world is watching! Well, maybe not the whole world, but at least our parents, and probably even some people on Earth. Watching the pod, I mean. With their telescopes. From space. Until we go behind Mars." Her words were coming out a jumble. The other humans were as confused as I was.

"Sorry," she said, slowing down. "What I mean is that they're probably observing us, right now, to see if we're okay. So even if the radio doesn't work, we could send them a message with—"

"Morse code!" cried Hollins.

"Exactly," said Nicki. "We can blink the lights of the pod on and off to send them a message that we're running out of air. Maybe they could send someone sooner. It's worth a shot."

"Okay, I think my dad had an old book about Morse code around here somewhere," said Hollins. "In the meantime, let's get our spacesuits on. If something else goes wrong, we don't want to be caught flat-footed."

"What else could go wrong?" asked Little Gus.

"Plenty of stuff," said Nicki cheerfully. "The computer could be overestimating the amount of air we have left. There could be an electrical fire. An aftershock from the quake could shake the pod to—"

She noticed that all the other humans were scowling at her.

"Sorry," she said. "Thinking out loud again."

CHAPTER TWELVE

The air in the pod had long since run out, now replaced by the surface atmosphere of Gelo. I sat on the floor of the sideways room, still tied, with the four humans. They had all put on their spacesuits several hours earlier. At first, they were eager to talk among themselves. They were close enough to actually hear each other without the use of their radios, though the glass of their helmets and the thinner atmospheric composition gave their voices a muffled, far-away quality. For the past hour or so, though, no one had said anything.

Even the computer voice, so eager to remind the humans of their impending doom, had fallen silent. After the air had run out, it probably assumed that all sensible humans had evacuated.

The young humans had sent their message. They'd

located the book, and then Nicki had used another holo-gram computer device, this one belonging to Hollins. She'd plugged it into the wall and reprogrammed the ship's lighting controls. Instead of flying saucers, the holographic display had shown a floating stream of human computer code that Nicki manipulated and changed. Apparently the devices weren't just for games.

Now, periodically, the lights of the pod would flick on and off according to an ancient human code of dots and dashes that represented characters in their alphabet. If someone was observing from space, and they knew this code, they might have gotten the following message:

"SOS. ONLY THREE HOURS AIR LEFT. SOS."

For a while, the blinking lights kept repeating this mes-sage (with Nicki periodically revising the number in the middle downward). Eventually the air had run out, and so it was shortened to simply:

"SOS."

The humans had each collected a few things in airtight bags: food, water, small illumination devices, more of the rope they'd used to restrain me, and Hollins's folding knife. They'd gathered these things as if they meant to take them somewhere, but it was unclear where they planned to go.

I'd gleaned that this was the pod where Hollins had lived

with his two originators—the fact that all humans apparently have two originators struck me as incredibly bizarre
and disturbing. I was morbidly curious, and I wanted to ask
them more about this. But I didn't quite have the language
skill, and frankly it seemed like the wrong time.

Every so often, the whole world would rattle and shake
for a few moments. Aftershocks from the quake. Each time
the rumbling would raise the young humans' hope: Perhaps
their mothership was landing nearby. Each time those hopes
were dashed.

"They're not coming," said Becky at last. Her voice was
faint, barely a whisper.

"Don't say that," said Hollins. "They'll come back. My
mom won't leave us here."

"Why didn't she override the automatic quarantine?"
Becky began.

Nicki cut her off. "Does it really matter, Becky? We're
here now. That's all." Becky shrugged and went silent again.

"I never even got to see Paris," said Little Gus.

"Did you want to see Paris?" asked Nicki.

"Not really," said Little Gus glumly. "That makes me
sad too. Why didn't I want to see Paris? Is something wrong
with me?"

"C'mon, let's send the message again," said Hollins.

Nicki plugged her hologram device into the wall, and the lights flicked off and on in the now familiar pattern. Three short blinks. Three long blinks. Three more short. SOS.

The humans were trying their best to deny the obvious. In a little while, the oxygen tanks on their spacesuits would be out of air as well. Despair was creeping in.

"Can help," I said, breaking the silence. Becky glared at me. At this point I knew what was coming next. My offer would be met with an argument, an accusation, a declaration of my obviously hostile intentions.

"How?" she said instead. "How can you help?"

"Have air," I said. "Have human air."

I'd made a decision. I couldn't just leave these humans to suffocate. If I hadn't sneaked aboard their pod, they would be up there between the stars. Headed home. Safe. Among their own kind.

It was my fault they were here.

Our two species might very well be at war now. But these four were my responsibility. I wasn't going to let them die.

CHAPTER THIRTEEN

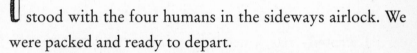

I stood with the four humans in the sideways airlock. We were packed and ready to depart.

I had told them, in halting human, that I could guide them to the cavern entrance near Jehe Canyon—where I'd seen them racing before. Once inside, they would be able to breathe the oxygen-rich air without their spacesuits.

At least this is what I hoped that I had said to them. I was learning their language quickly, but I was still only able to string a few difficult-to-pronounce human words together at a time. To me, human speech still sounded a bit like usk-lizards making territorial grunts.

Mercifully, I had been untied. Though I was informed in no uncertain terms, by both Hollins and Becky, that I was still their prisoner. Now possibly a "prisoner of war," in fact. Which sounded much worse to me.

"They can both be kind of bossy, huh?" said Little Gus, when he and I were alone for a moment. Nicki overheard and nodded knowingly.

"My whole thing is just chill, you know?" he said. I didn't know. But I nodded anyway.

My only request of the humans was that we bring all the remaining boxes of Feeney's Original Astronaut Ice Cream with us. Perhaps it was unfair of me to ask anything of them, since I had gotten them into this predicament and they were in no position to refuse. But honestly, I didn't care. I wanted—nay, I needed—to eat more of those delicious pink treats.

As it turned out, they had two unopened packages in addition to the one I had, er, sampled—and Little Gus had fallen on. I offered to carry all three boxes. To be helpful.

"We have to let our families know what happened," said Becky. She attached a handwritten note to the wall of the airlock. It explained the situation—why the humans were leaving the pod and where they were going. It included a crude map—that the young humans had drawn with my guidance—pointing toward the cavern entrance where I planned to take them.

I felt torn about leaving the human race a map to the Gelo cavern system, but I saw no other way. I realized I would likely face many similar ethical dilemmas if I was going to help these young humans survive.

"All right. Time to go," said Hollins. He pushed the glowing orange button, and the inner door of the airlock slowly rolled closed. Then the outer door opened. There was no whoosh this time. The air inside was the same as the air outside. The blue-gray surface of Gelo stretched out beyond us.

"Sound doesn't carry far in this atmosphere," said Hollins. "So we'll need to be on communicators once we're out there. Try not to talk much. Let's conserve battery power." I reactivated the tiny Nyrt-Snooper still in my ear.

Hollins hopped onto one of the four rocket-bikes in the airlock. "I'm the best pilot," he said, "so I'll take the lead."

"Wait a second," said Becky. "You're not the best pilot. Everyone knows I am."

"Becky, you remember the emergency flight training course we did in preparation for this mission? I shouldn't tell you this, but I got rated ninety-four percent."

"I was rated a ninety-seven percent," said Becky, smiling.

"Yo, I got a twenty-two percent," said Little Gus quietly. "That's still pretty good, right?"

"Not really," said Nicki, but no one seemed to hear her.

"Look, we could debate this all day," said Hollins to Becky. "Even if we are both equally good pilots—"

"Ninety-four and ninety-seven aren't equal," she snapped.

"Becky, my mom was the commander—"

"Meaning what, exactly?"

"I'm thirteen. You're only twelve. I'm nine months and twenty-two days older than you. So that means I'm the leader," said Hollins petulantly. Maybe he was still sore about losing the rocket-bike race to her?

"They're always like this," said Little Gus, shrugging. "It's like 'get married already.'"

"What? They are not going to get married!" cried Nicki. It was the most animated I'd ever seen her.

"We are not going to get married!" said Hollins and Becky in unison. Hollins's voice crackled high.

"What is 'married'?" I asked. No one had a very good answer for me. Apparently it was a legal and emotional union between two humans who specifically were not originator and offspring—the two adult Hollinses I'd seen earlier were an example. Beyond that, the humans got a little evasive.

"Why are we wasting time explaining this to it!" said Becky, exasperated.

"It? It has a name, you know," said Little Gus. "Wait . . . you do have a name, right?"

"I am Chorkle," I said.

"Whew!" said Little Gus. "I was worried it was going to be something crazy like 'Zhalufaxdyn' or 'Ranvonmo the Eternal.' Chorkle. That's easy enough to say."

"Pleased to meet you, Chorkle," said Nicki, and she extended her hand.

"Pleased to meet you," I said and waited. Her hand was still out. At last I grudgingly handed her a Feeney's Original Astronaut Ice Cream bar. She looked confused and then handed it back to me. That was good. I really hadn't wanted to give her one.

"Since we only have four bikes, Chorkle can ride with me," said Little Gus, clapping me on the back. I suddenly recalled watching him wreck his rocket-bike a dozen times when I'd observed these humans before. I didn't want to end up a Chorkle-colored stain on some jagged rocks.

"Maybe should ride with Hollins," I said, "as guide."

"Good point," said Hollins. "Hop on the back." I climbed onto the rocket-bike behind him and grasped him around the trunk.

"Everyone ready?" said Hollins, firing up the ignition of his rocket-bike.

"I kind of have to go to the bathroom," said Nicki.

"No time. Just go in your spacesuit," said Little Gus.

"They all have automatic waste-processing capability."

"What?" said Becky. "No they don't." Everyone stared at Little Gus.

"Oh. Huh," he said. "Oops."

"Hang on, Chorkle," said Hollins. And I did.

There was a roar. Then we were hurtling across the asteroid's surface at an impossible speed. Rocks and craters flashed past us in a blur. Hollins kept the rocket-bike steady with his hands on the pronged steering mechanism.

Sometimes we'd swerve left or right to avoid an obstacle. Sometimes Hollins would give the bike a little altitude and we'd sail right over a boulder at the last possible instant. It was thrilling and terrifying at once, like some sort of a real-life hologram game.

Just then another rocket-bike started to nose past. It was Becky, a broad grin spread across her face. She was turning this into another race.

Hollins leaned forward and punched the accelerator, and we went even faster. But Becky was still ahead of us. I clung onto Hollins for dear life. I looked back. Far behind us, I saw Nicki shaking her head.

"Becky, slow down! What are you doing?" said Hollins over their communicators.

"It's called 'piloting,'" she radioed back. "Don't worry.

I can teach you." She actually sounded happy for the first time since the pod had crashed.

Becky pulled dramatically into Jehe Canyon a few seconds before Hollins.

"Wow, glad you finally made it," she laughed. "I was getting bored."

"That was totally irresponsible," yelled Hollins. "This is an emergency situation. Now is not the time to goof off."

"Sorry, what did you say? I don't speak loser," said Becky. I had understood Hollins, so I felt a burst of pride that I apparently did speak loser.

At last Nicki arrived in the canyon.

"Guys, splitting up the group and traveling at high speed for no reason is kind of dangerous," said Nicki. "You know that, right?" From the looks on their faces and their mumbled responses, they both knew that.

Little Gus pulled up a little while later. His rocket-bike had a fresh dent in it, and his spacesuit was covered in dust.

"Good thing you weren't riding with me, Chorkle," said Little Gus, rubbing his neck, "This rock came out of nowhere, and wham! I think I fractured my, uh . . . this bone right here."

"Clavicle?" said Nicki.

"Gross, Nicki," said Little Gus.

"Okay, so where do we find these caves?" said Hollins to me.

And so I brought four humans to the hidden entrance to the real Gelo.

CHAPTER FOURTEEN

Before I took them below, I encouraged the humans to conceal their rocket-bikes as best they could.

"Couldn't we use them to get around in the caves?" asked Nicki.

"Yeah. Beats walking," said Becky.

"Not inside," I said. "Too narrow." The rocket bikes were too big for most of the winding confines of the tunnel system.

The humans ended up stashing all four of them inside a nearby crater. They were invisible unless you were looking down from above or actually standing inside the crater itself. It wasn't a perfect hiding spot, but it was better than nothing.

"So where is this entrance?" asked Hollins.

I found a thoroughly ordinary blue-gray Gelo rock and

reached behind it, fiddling around a bit. There was a click and then a hiss as it swung open to reveal a dark tunnel behind it.

The four humans followed me inside, and I closed the hatch behind us with a dull clank.

"My home," I said.

Their eyes slowly adjusted to the gloom. Then their mouths fell open. We stood in a cavern that snaked its way downward, toward the heart of the asteroid. The walls and floor were covered with countless species of mushrooms and lichens and molds. Bulbous phosphorescent globules—fungus that we Xotonians call glowing zhas—provided enough dim greenish light for the humans to see.

"Dude. This. Place. Is. Super. Weird," said Little Gus, slowly reaching out to touch a feathery sicras-stalk growing out of the rocks. The sicras-stalk recoiled from his hand, startling him.

It struck me how strange these caverns—utterly familiar to me—must seem to a typical human. They'd all been born and raised on the bright blue-and-green surface of Eo.

"We thought this asteroid was totally lifeless," said Hollins, shaking his head in disbelief. "I guess we were just focused on looking for iridium."

"I have to collect samples!" cried Nicki. And she ran to

the walls and began picking one of each type of fungus and carefully storing it inside an individual plastic baggie. Fascinated by fungi. She and Linod would probably get along well.

"Nicki, come on," said Becky. "Those things are disgusting." But from her tone I could tell she held little hope of dissuading her duplicate in this matter.

The humans were still wearing their spacesuits. Hollins checked the meter on his belt.

"Only thirty minutes of oxygen left," he sighed.

"Air here breathable . . . for humans," I reiterated. This was the reason I'd brought them here. Becky and Hollins looked at each other.

"If you're wrong about this . . ." said Becky to me, crossing her arms.

"We'll all suffocate to death horribly," added Nicki helpfully. She noticed that everyone was staring at her. "What? If we want it to learn proper grammar, we have to speak in complete sentences."

"Maybe bringing us here to suffocate was its plan all along?" said Becky. That would have been a very complicated and time-consuming plan, I thought, considering I could have just as easily let them die in their own pod.

I didn't share this, of course. Instead I said, "Not plan."

"Too late to worry about it now," said Hollins. "We have no choice but to trust Chorkle. If I pass out, try to re-pressurize my suit and wake me up."

"Pass out?" said Little Gus. "Wait, Hollins, maybe we should—"

Hollins cut him off. "Here goes nothing," he said. In one final act of not quite total trust, he took a big breath of air. Then he popped the seal on his spacesuit's helmet.

He slowly lifted the helmet off his head, still holding his breath. Everyone stared at him in agonizing silence. I suddenly started to worry that I'd incorrectly judged how much oxygen these humans actually needed to live.

Hollins's skin took on a bluish tinge. He began to tap his foot. At last he gasped and sucked in a big breath of Gelo cavern atmosphere. His face looked terrified. Gradually his breathing slowed to normal. His fear gave way to a smile. He gave the others a nod, and one by one they popped off their helmets as well.

They all began to laugh. Little Gus danced around and burst into an impromptu song about how cool breathing is.

"Chorkle, you did it!" cried Nicki, and she wrapped both her arms around me and squeezed. "So the air in these caverns must be at least seventeen percent oxygen, right?"

"Uh," I said.

"An alien best friend," said Little Gus, trying to pick me up but toppling us both over. "Everybody in sixth grade is going to be so jealous. Might even impress a few seventh graders."

"This still doesn't make up for causing our pod to crash," said Becky.

"Come on, Becky," said Hollins. "Ease up. Credit where credit is due. Thank you, Chorkle. You saved our lives. You're still a prisoner, though."

"Thanks, alien," said Becky quietly. She still sounded angry.

The truth is, Becky was right. I'd solved the most pressing of the humans' problems; they weren't going to run out of air. So what? It still didn't make up for stranding them here.

"Chorkle, are there any others of your kind?" asked Hollins. Now that the immediate danger had passed, he was already trying to think of the next step of their plan. "Maybe they could fly us back to our parents."

"Xotonians not have starship," I said.

"Maybe there's another way they could—"

"Others not . . . understand humans," I said. I was trying not to scare anyone.

There was no way I could take them to Core-of-Rock. I could only imagine what Sheln—and all the others who

111

favored a direct attack on the humans—might do if I brought these four back home with me. In fact, now the greatest danger to these humans was probably running into an angry mob of Xotonians in the tunnels.

And if I'm being truly honest, there was another, more selfish reason I didn't want to go home: Kalac. If I hadn't sneaked aboard the human pod, the asteroid-quake plan would have gone off without a hitch, and the humans would now be gone from our world.

Instead I'd stranded these four on our asteroid and, even worse, allowed myself to be seen by the human commander. By now, probably all twelve billion humans knew that Gelo was inhabited. It sounded like the humans were going to return with soldiers to reclaim their offspring. Like Becky, Kalac had every right to be furious with me. I just couldn't face that.

I tried to tell myself my intentions had been good, but it didn't change a thing.

It was up to me to get the young humans back to their families and somehow avert a war between our two peoples. If by some miracle I could solve both those monumental problems—unlikely, considering I had no good ideas for either of them—only then would it be safe for me to return home.

"So what do we do now?" asked Nicki. She'd collected one of every fungus in the immediate area. She was already straining under the weight of her duffle bag.

"Keep moving," I said. "Moving . . . safe." That last part of what I said might not have been technically true. I probably should have said "safer." But again, I didn't want to frighten them. And I did need to take them someplace where other Xotonians wouldn't find them.

"Follow," I said.

We walked a hundred meters until we came to a fork in the passage. A right-hand turn was the first of the twenty-seven that would lead us to Core-of-Rock.

I turned left. I was taking them deeper into the Un-claimed Tunnels.

CHAPTER FIFTEEN

"So much of the life in these caverns apparently requires no sunlight at all," said Nicki while scraping at a green . . . something on the rocks. "It's interesting. This is the only species I've seen that seems to engage in any sort of photosynthesis whatsoever. And it apparently relies on the light from the glowing zhas—not the sun!"

"Yes, that is interesting," I lied.

According to my chronometer, we'd been traveling through the Unclaimed Tunnels for over a day now. Nicki's sense of scientific wonder was undiminished. As fascinating as I found all things human, she was even more interested in learning everything about my subterranean world.

She held up a tiny piece of the green something with a pair of tweezers. "I mean, what do you even call this stuff?"

"I . . . I don't know," I said. "It doesn't have a name. You can name it."

Her face lit up. "Well, I've been referring to most of what we've seen growing down here as 'fungi' because of certain apparent similarities to organisms we have on Earth," she said. "But obviously, any life on this asteroid evolved completely separately from life on Earth. I mean, unless you believe in exogenesis or something."

Here, she paused as though she expected a response from me. I shrugged.

"We might need a whole new kingdom of biological classification!" she said. "Probably more than one, even." Her words were tumbling out of her mouth now, as they always seemed to when she got excited.

"Then, of course, we would have to come up with its phylum, class, order, family, and genus. It would take years of study," she said, now frowning at the problem of the anonymous green speck. "Giving it a proper scientific name at this time is impossible."

"Why don't you just call it 'Little-Gus-Is-the-Original-King'?" said Little Gus, strolling up to us. "It's simple. Easy to remember. Rolls off the tongue."

"I think that name would be confusing," said Nicki, distractedly making handwritten notes about the green something, "but I'll take it under advisement."

"Anyway, dinner's ready," said Little Gus. Despite being the youngest of the humans, he had assumed the role of the group's cook. It wasn't so much that he was good at cooking; it was more that the other three were terrible at it. Personally, I couldn't tell much difference. The only human food I cared to eat was astronaut ice cream. After that nothing ever tasted sweet enough.

"Tonight we're having Little Gus Stew, piping hot!" said Little Gus. I was starting to detect a recurring theme as to how he chose to name things. The group had eaten Little Gus Eggs that morning.

"What is Little Gus Stew?" I asked as the three of us walked back toward our camp.

"Simple recipe. Take all your dehydrated food and mix it together. Then add water and heat it over an open flame until it turns from gray to dark gray," he said. "Of course, the secret ingredient is love."

We walked beside a huge underground lake that seemed to stretch on forever. This lake had no name that I knew of. We were far into the Unclaimed Tunnels now. Fifty-nine turns from Core-of-Rock, if we retraced our steps.

This was an area where Xotonians rarely traveled—which is exactly why I had brought us here. The occasional hunter or forager or scout might pass through these deserted caverns. But the entirety of our small civilization was located at Core-of-Rock. Almost all our food, water, and other necessities were produced within the protection of the Stealth Shield. According to Hudka, this too was by Jalasu Jhuk's design.

Hudka. The thought of my grand-originator gave me a pang of homesickness. I'd been gone for nearly two days now. Hudka was probably worried about me. At least it had some idea of where I'd gone, I tried to tell myself. Maybe Hudka was sitting at home running up its own high score in Xenostryfe III. Wishful thinking, probably.

While I missed Hudka, I dreaded the thought of seeing Kalac. I couldn't imagine how disappointed and angry my originator would be.

So far, our journey through the Unclaimed Tunnels had been a slow one. In many ways humans were not well suited to subterranean travel.

These juveniles were a bit taller than even the average adult Xotonian, and, owing to their strange body structure, they often had a hard time squeezing through narrow passages.

They had difficulty even walking in this environment, especially across cavern floors that were smooth and slick with water and fine silt. Every so often, one of them would fall and land on their backside. If it didn't look too painful, the others would laugh.

Early on in the journey, Nicki had slipped off a narrow ledge and slid thirty meters down a steep, mud-covered slope. Luckily, she hadn't been seriously hurt. But her bag had been open at the time, and a good bit of the human food supply had fallen out of it and into a deep crevasse—a space so narrow that even I couldn't retrieve it. She was much more concerned with all her biological samples that had been lost. After the incident, Hollins instituted a policy that all the humans should be tethered together when walking.

"This way, if one of us falls, the others can hold them up," he said after they'd tied a rope around all their waists.

"More like if one of us falls, we take all the others with us," grumbled Becky. Again, I wasn't sure she was wrong.

Light was also an issue. The glowing zhas is an extremely common species, and it bathes most caverns in a dim, greenish light, about as bright as twilight on Eo, according to the humans.

But there are some tunnels where there is no glowing zhas. And in those places, human eyes were totally useless.

"Try to dilate your pupils further," I said to them after we'd reached one such darkened area, "to let more light in."

"We can't 'try' to do that," said Becky. "Our pupils just dilate on their own."

"Then your species needs more eyes," I grumbled.

"You know, that's a really good idea," said Nicki, attempting to jot something down in her notebook despite her inability to see. Presumably she'd had a thought about how to increase the human eyeball count.

In the deepest darkness, the humans had no choice but to pull out their small illumination devices—"flashlights," as they were called—to light their way. These flashlights were annoying to me because their brightness made it impossible for me to see into the darkest corners of the caverns.

Occasionally, one of the humans would accidentally shine the beam right into my light-sensitive eyes, causing me a moment of excruciating pain and rendering me temporarily blind.

I begged them to please watch where they pointed those things. I needed my eyes. There was no shortage of dangers— Xotonian or otherwise—to watch out for in the Unclaimed Tunnels.

I was carefully avoiding the somewhat heedless beam of Little Gus's flashlight as we arrived at our camp on the shore of the lake—which, of course, had been christened "Little Gus Lake." The humans spread out their bedrolls on a small peninsula jutting a few dozen meters out into the calm black water.

A metal pot steamed over a little fire. Fragrant Little Gus Stew bubbled inside it. The humans figured out fairly quickly that fires were only a good idea in large caves with proper ventilation. Otherwise the smoke made breathing impossible.

"That acrid burning smell means it's almost done," said Little Gus as he began to stir the stew.

Nicki sat down and began quietly classifying. By now, she'd nearly refilled her bag with samples, almost too many to carry.

Hollins's hologram device—the same model as the one I had, er, borrowed from Nicki—sat tantalizingly on a nearby rock.

"Is that a human hologram device?" I asked, feigning ignorance.

"Yeah, it's a Tunstall 24x Holodrive," she said. "I used to have one that I coded on sometimes. But I lost it."

"Why is it called a 'Tunstall 24x Holodrive'?" I asked, trying to change the subject.

"Well, 'holo' is from the word 'hologram.' And 'drive' is like a computer drive. And 'Tunstall' is a company that makes computers. I don't know about the '24x,' though.

Sometimes we just add numbers and x's to make things sound cooler, I guess," she said. "Anyway, it's pretty useless."

"Why?"

"Well, the ship was our only link to satellite service. So no Internet. I think Hollins has just been using it to make a map of the caverns we've been through."

"I wonder if it has any games on it," I said. "I mean, if you humans indeed play games on such devices, a question to which I don't know the answer. Obviously."

Nicki stared at me for a second. "Yeah, it has some games," she said, something in her eyes changing. I recognized the expression because I'd seen it on Hudka, probably even made it myself. It was the look of a hologram game addict.

"Here, let me show you," she said, "to give you a sense of what human culture is like." Nicki activated the device with a flick of her hand, and the three-dimensional menu floated in space before her.

"This one is called Super Mar—"

"How about that one?" I said, pointing to the flying saucer icon of the blast-the-aliens game.

"How do you know that's a game?" she asked.

"Er, just a guess. Is it one? I don't know," I said.

"Yeah. It's called Xenostryfe III," she said. "But . . . I don't know if we should play it."

"Why?"

"Well, I'm worried that you might find it, uh, offensive," said Nicki.

"It's all about blasting aliens to goop," said Little Gus from across the campfire.

"Well, uh, yeah. Basically," said Nicki.

"It's okay," I said. "This is not offensive."

"Good," said Nicki, relieved. "I'm not a violent person, but Xenostryfe is my favorite thing to do on a holodrive outside of coding. In fact, I've been working on a mod where you shoot at flying doughnuts instead of—"

"Choose two-player mode," I said, now dropping all pretense. I needed my hologram-game fix.

Each of us grabbed a holographic blaster, and we repelled a computerized alien invasion together. Our lasers wove a web of fiery death for all flying saucers. Nicki was amazing at the game. Though I must admit, I wasn't too bad myself. Final score: Nicki, 1,659,870; Chorkle, 1,659,842.

"Wow . . . it's almost like you played that game before," she said.

"Almost," I said.

"Wait, did Chorkle beat you at Xenostryfe?" asked Little Gus, amazed.

"Nope. My score was twenty-eight points higher," snapped Nicki, startling me.

It was unlike her. I momentarily wondered if I was actually talking to her duplicate. Had Becky stolen Nicki's vision lenses to play some elaborate trick on me?

But the outburst passed just as quickly as it had come, and she went back to placidly taking notes on her specimens.

"Is it rude to ask how you were duplicated?" I said.

"Not rude," said Nicki, a little uncomfortably. "So first off, we're twins. We weren't 'duplicated.' Except . . . we sort of were, I guess. See, with identical twins, the zygote splits into two separate embryos. . . ."

And she launched into an extended description of human reproduction, as disgusting as it was terrifying.

"Wow. Giving Chorkle the talk already?" said Hollins, thankfully interrupting the lecture. He and the real Becky had returned to camp together. Both of them held a coil of twine with a makeshift wire hook on the end.

"And just where were you two?" asked Nicki, her voice suddenly sharp again.

"Still trying to catch those reeya . . . er, ruhyee . . ." said Hollins, trying to remember the Xotonian word I'd taught him. His pronunciation was atrocious. As quickly as I had been picking up the human language—Nicki had described it as "linguistic hyperaptitude"—the humans were very slow to learn even the most rudimentary Xotonian.

"Chorkle, help me out here," he said at last.

"R'yaris," I said. He was searching for the word for the blind aquatic creatures common to the underground lakes of Gelo. They range in size from nearly microscopic to almost as large as a full-grown Xotonian.

"Right, reehaayrees . . . those fish-thingies," he said. "But I haven't had any luck."

"I'm not sure I'd want to eat a r'yari if we could catch one," said Becky. "I got a pretty good look at them. They're like brains that can swim."

"Heh, you're just mad because you didn't catch anything," said Hollins.

"Thanks for the psychoanalysis," said Becky. "But you didn't catch anything either, Dr. Freud."

"What is Dr. Freud?" I asked. No one answered.

"Yeah, I know. But it doesn't make me angry. It inspires me to do better. 'With self-discipline, most anything is possible.' Teddy Roosevelt," said Hollins smugly. "Tomorrow, I'm going to use a little bit of dehydrated beef for bait. I'll catch a ton of brain-fish."

"Care to make it interesting?" said Becky.

"What, like a bet?" said Hollins.

"Yup. When I catch more r'yaris tomorrow, then you have to carry my bag for a whole day."

"Sure," said Hollins. "But if I win, it wouldn't be chivalrous to make you carry my bag because you're a— "

"Oh please," said Becky. "I can carry your dumb bag, you loser."

"All right then, you're on," said Hollins.

"What if it's a tie?" I asked.

"It won't be a tie!" they both said in unison. They had a strange way of doing that.

"Anyway," said Hollins, "I'm going to gather some firewoo—sorry. Not wood. I meant, er, how do you say it? Fullud . . . fell— "

"Philiddra," I said. "Philiddra" was the Xotonian word for any of the varieties of tall mushrooms and fungi that sometimes grow in thick forests in the larger caverns of Gelo. The humans likened them to the "trees" of their own planet. I'd shown them how to burn their fallen branches to make a campfire.

"Right, what you said," he said. "Back in a few." And he walked off toward a nearby grove of them, whistling.

"So that's all you were doing?" said Nicki to Becky once Hollins was out of earshot. "Fishing? Or r'yari-ing? Or whatever the verb is?"

"Yes! Calm down. That's all we were doing," cried Becky. "Sis, can you try not to be insane? Look, I brought you back one of these." Becky handed her a small, wilted mushroom.

"I already have a dozen of those," snapped Nicki. "They're called nosts, and they're probably the most common, boring species down here! Anyway, this is a terrible sample." She flicked the nost over her shoulder.

"Come on, Nicki," said Becky, shrugging. "You can't expect me to know which ones are boring and which ones aren't."

Nicki made a sort of harrumph noise and stalked off.

"Seriously? You're mad at me? What did I do?" said Becky. "You're supposed to be levelheaded. I'm the unreasonable one!" And she followed her duplicate.

"Yo, where is everybody going?" asked Little Gus. "I told you that dinner is ready. The Little Gus Stew is just starting to congeal." No one answered.

"Eh. More for us," he said to me, slopping a steaming gray spoonful into a bowl. "I like the skin on top the best."

"Why are the duplicates fighting?" I asked Little Gus, poking at his eponymous stew.

"Twins," said Little Gus. "We call them 'twins.'"

"Right, 'twins,'" I said. "If, as Nicki explained, they have

126

virtually identical genetic material, then shouldn't they . . . agree more often?"

"Oh, Chorkle," he said, shaking his head, "I think they're fighting because they do agree on something."

"I don't understand," I said.

"It's the simplest reason in the whole universe." He smiled and pointed his spoon toward Hollins, carrying a load of philiddra branches back toward camp.

"You've got a lot to learn about humans, my little friend," said Little Gus.

CHAPTER SIXTEEN

We made our way up a steep tunnel. The path was thick with a fungus that we Xotonians call spiny dralts. In some places it grew as high as the humans' waists. Spiny dralts are covered in long thorns. These thorns had a tendency to prick sensitive human skin wherever it was exposed.

I kept a bit ahead, scouting for obstacles or danger, trying to pick the easiest route for the group. Every so often I'd hear a loud "Ow!" or "Ah!" or any of a few other human words—words that all of them told me not to repeat too often. I would look back to see one of the humans sucking on a finger or waving a hand around that they'd accidentally spiked with a wicked dralt thorn.

The humans were still tethered together with their safety rope, which meant they could only move as fast as the slowest walker. Usually this was Little Gus, whose legs were shorter than those of the others. But other times it was just whoever happened to be the most tired. And the humans got tired often. I wasn't even tethered to them, but I was still limited to their plodding pace.

When we reached the top of a rise in the tunnel, all four humans begged for a rest.

"Strange how the alien is the prisoner, but we're the ones tied up and being led around," grumbled Becky.

"Kind of a fair point," said Hollins. "Where are we anyway, Chorkle?"

"We are in the Unclaimed Tunnels," I said, dodging his question. We weren't lost exactly—one hundred twenty-one turns back to Core-of-Rock—but I had no idea where we were. I'd never been in these caverns before. Even the fungi looked different here.

"Why do we have to keep walking?" asked Becky. "Where are we even going?" She sat on a rock, rubbing her foot.

"It is safest to keep moving," I said.

"What if we just relaxed here for a while?" asked Little Gus. He slowly leaned back, his eyelids drooping. "Maybe we could take a fifteen-minute—ow!"

Suddenly he was wide awake, sitting upright and rubbing his neck. He'd accidentally brushed against a spiny dralt.

"Dude. Is there anything on this asteroid that doesn't want to kill us?" he asked.

"Me," I said, shrugging.

"Debatable," said Becky.

"It's been nearly three days," said Nicki. "Our parents will be coming back soon. If they can't find us, they might assume the worst."

"We should have stayed near the entrance to the surface," said Becky.

"No, it would not have been safe," I said. "That entrance is well traveled. Very dangerous." The Xotonian Observers who watch the sky must have seen the pod's emergency landing. Others would probably be investigating the site by now. That would mean a lot of coming and going by the entrances nearest to the human settlement. I couldn't risk it.

"You're worried about others finding us. I get that," said Hollins, reading my mind. "But we can't just keep on walking around forever. We're running out of food."

He was right on both counts. Unfortunately, I hadn't come up with a better plan yet. Leading them to breathable air had earned me a certain amount of trust with the humans. Now I could see that trust was starting to wear thin.

"Chorkle, are there any other Xotonians like you?" asked Nicki. "Who would give humans the benefit of the doubt? Who would help us get back to our parents? Maybe we could find them somehow and—"

"I do not understand," I lied.

"Really?" asked Nicki. "You somehow learned our whole language in a couple of days, but suddenly you don't understand what I'm asking?"

"I do not understand," I said, and I shook my head and shrugged and tried to seem as stupid as possible. Nicki looked skeptical.

There probably were a few Xotonians who wouldn't want to kill these humans on sight—Hudka, for one. Linod too. But enlisting their help meant returning to Core-of-Rock, back to where Kalac was. I was terrified at the thought of explaining myself—especially my role in botching the asteroid-quake plan and potentially endangering our entire species—to my originator. Kalac would probably disown me.

So we continued onward. After a few more hours of walking, the tunnel began to widen and descend. Its contours became less irregular.

"Hey, what is this?" asked Nicki during another rest. She had scraped a bit of yellow mold from the cavern wall.

I was about tell her that I had no idea, that it was impossible for anyone to know the name of every single fungus we passed and would she please stop asking. But it wasn't the mold she was talking about. It was what was behind it.

Carved into the cavern wall was an intricate . . . fixture of some sort, a regular star-shaped hole surrounded by patterned carving.

"Did Xotonians make this?" asked Nicki.

"I think so," I said. It did look Xotonian to me. But it seemed older somehow. After a bit of digging on the floor beneath it, Little Gus found a shard of transparent crystal. We all began to look for more—an excuse for the humans to prolong their break. One by one, we found more shards and fit them back into the fixture on the cavern wall. It was like a kind of puzzle. At last Becky completed the star by popping the last broken piece of crystal in.

And all of a sudden, the star bathed the tunnel around it in a soft, yellow glow. It was a wall light.

"Chorkle, are you sure nobody lives here?" asked Little Gus, looking around nervously. The caverns were silent, save for the distant sound of dripping water. It looked to me like the fixture hadn't been touched in hundreds of years.

"Yes, I'm sure," I said. But just in case, I popped the crystal pieces out of the wall, dimming the cavern once more.

"I'd say from the amount of mold, whoever made it

is long dead," said Nicki. "The real question is what—or who—killed them?" Everyone frowned at her.

"Sorry," she said quietly. "I was just thinking out loud. . . ."

Now as we walked, we all began to notice identical fixtures on the cavern walls. Some were broken. Others were worn away or almost entirely covered. They seemed to appear at regular intervals.

The undergrowth of spiny dralts soon began to thin—much to the humans' relief—and we came to the entrance of a huge chamber. A gnarled forest of philiddra grew here. Their branches blocked most of the light from the glowing zhas on the ceiling high above and cast strange shadows upon the cavern floor. Curls of mist hung in the air between their trunks.

"You've been here before, right?" said Hollins, shining his flashlight out into the dark chamber.

"Of course," I lied. In truth, even I found this place eerie. I couldn't imagine how the humans might feel.

"Nicki, say you're in a place—hypothetically, let's say an asteroid—where there aren't any people. Is it scientifically possible for there to be ghosts?" asked Little Gus, his light darting around.

"I think it's unlikely that ghosts exist. But the universe

is so complex, I wouldn't say impossible," said Nicki. "For example, we didn't believe there were aliens until—"

"Come on, sis," said Becky. "You're scaring him."

"But if you accept the proposition of human ghosts—which, as I said before, I don't—then it wouldn't be illogical to assume that the Xotonians have their own restless dead spirits," said Nicki.

"Nobody needs to worry about ghosts," said Hollins. But his voice sounded uneasy.

We pushed onward into the forest. The humans were keeping closer together now. The weak beams of their flashlights were soon lost in the mist.

We came upon a mound covered in thick rust-colored mildew, a loose pile of stones in a circular shape. As we got closer it became apparent to me: This had once been a dome-shaped Xotonian building.

I spotted something dark among the stones. Using a fel'graz, I gently brushed aside the dirt and detritus.

It was a charred Xotonian skull!

Startled, I somersaulted backward and collided with Hollins.

"Whoa!" said Hollins, lifting me back to my fel'grazes. "Hope that wasn't a friend of yours."

We saw more mounds now. Here and there, a blackened,

crumbling wall still stood among the philiddra. The occasional broken stone column jutted out of the ground, worn almost as smooth as a stalagmite. This strange forest was growing in the ruins of what must have been a second Xotonian settlement.

We were many turns from Core-of-Rock—at least, if we retraced our steps. I had never heard of Xotonians building anything outside the Stealth Shield—not even from Hudka, who loved to dwell on the past. If the elders knew of these ruins, they hadn't bothered to tell us younglings about it.

Perhaps it was the dreary atmosphere of the forest, but the mood of the group became glum and anxious. We set up camp in silence, beside a river that snaked its way across the chamber's floor. It wasn't wide, but it was deeper than it looked. Pale r'yaris flitted about below the water's surface.

In an effort to boost morale, Hollins reminded Becky of their r'yari fishing bet.

"I'm going to get that fat one right there," said Hollins, pointing to a large r'yari near the surface. "Mmm-mmm. That's good eatin'."

"Whatever, Hollins," said Becky. "I'm tired and I don't care. I concede. You win." She seemed particularly sullen. It wasn't like her to shrink from a challenge.

Hollins was a little taken aback. "Don't worry," he said. "I'll catch at least twenty. I don't mind sharing one with you, if you ask nicely. Dehydrated beef is the secret!" he said as he pulled a wad of brown flakes from a small silvery packet.

"Yo, don't waste that stuff!" said little Gus. "We're running out. Little Gus Stew won't be the same without it."

"Really?" said Hollins hopefully.

"I mean that it will be worse!" said Little Gus.

"Don't worry. I'm not wasting it," said Hollins. "I'm using it to get us more food. Force multiplier." And he walked off to find a prime r'yari fishing spot downstream.

"Speaking of Little Gus Stew, I need to find something to substitute for dehydrated potatoes. We're out of those too," said Little Gus.

"I think I saw some purple puffballs a little ways back," said Nicki.

"That sounds perfect!" said Little Gus, and the both of them disappeared the way we had come.

It was just Becky and me now. She sat on the ground, quiet and scowling.

"What's wrong?" I asked her.

"Great, now the alien wants to talk about feelings," said Becky to no one in particular.

"You know, to me, you are the alien," I said. "Your

people came here from outer space and started taking all the iridium."

"Yeah, I guess that was kind of crappy," she said at last. "We probably should have asked or something."

"It's okay," I said. "You didn't even know we were here. We were too scared to even show ourselves."

"I'm sorry I've been mean to you, Chorkle. I know you're trying to help us. It's just that I want to go home," she said. "I miss my parents and my friends and my planet. And I'm—I'm scared."

"I'm scared too," I said.

"Really?"

"But I can't go home. I disobeyed my origi—my 'parent.' I can't imagine how disappointed Kalac will be with me."

"I know what you mean," said Becky. "Both my parents are scientists. Which twin do you think they're more proud of?"

"Maybe you could wear a pair of vision lenses and then they wouldn't be able to tell the two of you apart," I offered.

She laughed. "I'm not sure that would work for long, Chorkle. Fact is, I love my parents more than anything, but I'm not going to be a scientist like they are. I want to be a pilot. Or a reporter. Or a combination pilot-reporter. Sooner or later, they'll just have to accept that."

"Do you think Kalac will accept my mistakes? Forgive me for messing up everything?"

She placed a hand lightly on my thol'graz. "Of course. I think going your own way is just part of growing up," she said. "Otherwise, how would you figure out who you really are?"

Her words made me think of Hudka, always at odds with its own offspring. I'd never really considered it before, but Kalac must have sometimes defied and disappointed Hudka when it was younger. As much as I loved Hudka as a grand-originator, I could see that being its direct offspring could not have been easy.

I thought too of how caring Kalac could be, carrying me on its i'ardas when I was younger, taking me to the market for a fried cave slug, checking under my sleeping-veth to make sure Morool wasn't hiding in the shadows.

"It must be hard for our parents to see us grow up," I said.

"Yup," said Becky. "Hard for us too. Because growing up doesn't just mean doing whatever we want to do. It's also doing what we have to do. Even when we're afraid."

She was right. I knew that I would have to return to Core-of-Rock and face my mistakes.

"I think I know how you can win," I said.

"Win what?"

"Your bet with Hollins. To catch more r'yaris."

"Do tell." She was actually smiling now.

"There is a bait that might be a bit more effective than dehydrated beef," I said. And I pulled out a silvery bar of Feeney's Original Astronaut Ice Cream.

CHAPTER SEVENTEEN

"Got another bite," said Becky as her fishing line tightened. She had already caught five r'yaris. I must admit, wriggling on dry land, they did look a bit like brains that could swim.

"Seriously?" called Hollins from the other side of the river (he'd crossed using a dead philiddra trunk as a bridge). "How are you doing this?" Hollins had yet to catch anything at his "prime spot."

"Just a simple combination of skill, talent, and dedication," said Becky. Neither Becky nor I had let him in on the little secret of using astronaut ice cream as bait. As predicted, the r'yaris loved it as much as I did. After all, astronaut ice cream was the most delicious thing in the entire universe.

"Don't worry. I'm sure you'll catch something someday," said Becky. "Just keep at it. Never give up. Follow your dreams. Stay in school. Winners don't use drugs. Teddy Roosevelt said that."

"No, he didn't," said Hollins quietly.

"Whoa!" said Becky as the pole—the thin, flexible stalk of a young philiddra with a line tied to the end of it—was nearly yanked from her hands. The r'yari she had hooked was struggling violently. Becky was having a hard time pulling it in.

"Wow, that looks like a really big one," said Nicki, staring into the churning water. The r'yari really did appear to be about twice the size of the others she'd caught, the biggest I'd ever seen.

"Maybe this one is their king," said Little Gus.

Both of them had come to the banks of the river to watch the fishing contest, which wasn't really much of a contest anymore. It gave the humans something to focus on, a welcome distraction from the creepiness of the surrounding forest and burned-out ruins.

"Come on, come on," said Becky, straining. Her pole was nearly doubled over now.

"I'm gonna fry that bad boy up and serve him with a side of warm dehydrated pickles. Little Gus style," said Little Gus as he watched it struggle.

"Careful, Becky," said Nicki, "it looks like your pole is about to—"

Snap! Becky's fishing pole broke in half, sending her flying backward. She flopped on the ground with a grunt. The top half of the pole, still attached to the line in the big r'yari's mouth, disappeared under the dark water of the river.

"It's okay," said Hollins, now needling Becky. "Even the best fisherman falls on his butt sometimes."

"Fisherwoman," said Becky, sitting up.

"Fisherperson," said Nicki.

"Wait, there it is!" I cried. The broken pole had resurfaced a few meters upstream. It bobbed there, near the bank.

"I probably shouldn't do this," said Little Gus, "but even I'm tired of eating nothing but stew." And he started to run toward the bank of the river.

"Wait, Gus! Becky already caught five of these things," said Hollins. "You don't need to—"

Little Gus leaped high into the air and disappeared beneath the water with a huge splash. We all stared at one another.

"We don't even know if r'yaris are edible or not," said Nicki, shaking her head.

At last, Gus popped up again.

"Got it!" he cried triumphantly. The broken pole was clutched in his hand.

"Dude, you're nuts," said Hollins.

"For the record, technically, that still counts as one that I caught," said Becky.

"Wow, it's pretty deep here," said Little Gus, treading water. "My feet don't even touch the bottom."

"Be careful," I said. "R'yaris are strong swimmers."

"Don't worry, Chorkle," said Little Gus, "I got everything under—"

Suddenly, the pole fragment violently yanked backward, pulling Little Gus along with it.

"Free ride!" said Little Gus.

"Come on, let go!" said Hollins. And he ran after Little Gus, who was now being rapidly towed upstream. We all followed close behind.

"Just let go of the pole!" cried Nicki.

"No way," laughed Little Gus, his head throwing up a wake as it sliced through the water. "This is awesome."

He was outpacing us now, receding into the distance. The little river was widening and becoming foamier and faster.

"Seriously, if you guys ever get a chance to have an oversized alien fish pull you down a river," cried Little Gus, his voice now faint, "I suggest you take it. Life's too short, you know."

"Gus, let go of the pole!" cried Hollins.

Little Gus yelled something back, but his voice was just

a murmur over the roar of the rushing water. His head was a red speck, intermittently visible on the uneven surface of the now rushing river.

"Oh no," said Nicki, and she pointed up ahead of us. Little Gus's head slipped out of sight. He'd gone over a waterfall!

We raced to the edge, Hollins on one bank, Nicki, Becky, and I on the other. Ten meters below us was a pool ringed with jagged rocks. Little Gus was nowhere to be seen.

Across the river, Hollins was frantically searching for some way down the cliff. Its surface was slippery and sheer, impossible for a human to climb.

"Humans can't breathe underwater, right?" I asked.

"No!" cried the duplicates.

"Then Little Gus needs help," I said.

"Yes!" they both screamed.

I took a deep breath. Then I somersaulted off the cliff and landed on a thin ledge halfway down. I somersaulted again and dove right into the pool. As I said, Xotonians are good climbers.

Unfortunately, we're terrible swimmers. I hit the water and flapped all four of my thol'grazes frantically. The pummeling force of the waterfall pushed me down to the bottom of the pool.

It was too cloudy to see much of anything, so I groped around blindly. Sometimes I'd grab a thol'graz full of silt. Sometimes nothing. Once I felt something disturbingly squishy. The waterfall was loud, even underneath the surface. I was starting to forget which way was up. Where was Little Gus? He must be down here somewhere.

Something flashed in front of my face. I reached for it but missed. I reached again and caught it. Desperately, I began to paddle in the direction that I thought was toward the surface and toward the shore, pulling whatever it was along with me.

I popped above the water, gasping. Somehow I was still holding on to what I'd found down there. It was a boot. Attached to a leg. I was holding Little Gus.

"You got him!" cried Becky from the top of the waterfall.

I pulled Little Gus onto a rocky shore a little further downstream and slumped to the ground beside him. I was thoroughly exhausted.

"Hollins went back to camp to get the rope," said Becky. "In the meantime, you need to check to see if Gus is breathing."

"How?" I said.

"Feel under his nose," said Nicki.

I did. Nothing. His skin had a bluish cast to it.

"I don't think he is," I yelled.

"Then you need to do mouth-to-mouth," yelled Nicki.

"What? I don't have a mouth," I yelled back. "I have a gul'orp!"

"Good enough!" cried Nicki. "Take a deep breath and put your . . . 'gul'orp' over his mouth. Then breathe out."

I did. Nothing.

"Do it again," cried Nicki.

I did. Nothing. Then a sputter. Little Gus sat up, coughing out river water. Nicki and Becky cheered from the top of the waterfall.

"Where am I?" asked Little Gus, dazed.

"In a river in a cavern on an asteroid called Gelo," I said.

"Cool," said Little Gus, still coughing. Slowly he sat up. He looked back at the waterfall.

"Did I go over that?"

"Yes," I said.

"Gus, are you okay?" yelled Nicki.

"I think so," he yelled back. "Maybe I should have let go of the fishing pole."

"You think?" asked Becky.

"Thanks, Chorkle," he said. "You saved my life. Again."

I shrugged.

On the shore around us were piles of fallen boulders and

more circular ruins of Xotonian buildings. Apparently this river had run right through the ancient settlement.

"Hey, check it out," said Little Gus, walking over to two rocks at the edge of the water. The broken half of the fishing pole was wedged between them. Little Gus grabbed the pole with both hands and pulled hard. With all his strength, he hefted a big wriggling r'yari—almost his size—right out of the water. It was thoroughly tangled up in the fishing line.

"Look!" he yelled triumphantly.

"Look!" cried Nicki.

"I know," said Little Gus. "That's what I'm saying: Look."

"No! Look!" screamed Becky. "Look behind you!"

Little Gus and I turned. Creeping out from among the rocks was a thyss-cat. And it looked hungry.

CHAPTER EIGHTEEN

Little Gus dropped the r'yari on the ground with a wet squelch. We both stood perfectly still as the thyss-cat crept toward us, muscles rippling under glossy blue fur. The big r'yari flopped around helplessly on the rocks by Gus's feet.

"Chorkle," he said very quietly, "what is that thing?"

"Thyss-cat," I whispered.

"And would you describe it as 'nice'? Or . . . 'not nice'?"

The thyss-cat is an apex predator in the subterranean ecosystem of Gelo. The top of the food chain. The king of the cavern. It is as big as three Xotonians put together. It can move in total silence. And it is powerful enough to bring down an usk-lizard by itself. The thyss-cat has six legs, each ending in five wicked claws, and jaws that are quite capable of crushing a Xotonian skull. Occasionally, it uses them for that very thing. The most common adage about the beast is that if you've seen one, it is already hunting you.

"Not nice," I said.

"Hey! Chorkle! Hey, where'd you go?" asked Little Gus. He kept his voice quiet, but he sounded terrified.

Unconsciously, my skin had camouflaged itself. It was an autonomic response to the threat of a nearby predator. I was now exactly the same shade as the mossy rocks around us. Had the thyss-cat seen me or not?

"Camouflaged," I said. "Don't move."

"Camouflaged? What am I supposed to do? I don't have any natural defenses," whimpered Little Gus. "I don't even have quills. . . ."

The thyss-cat moved toward us. It was close enough now that I could see the yellow slits of its eyes.

"I think—I think it wants to eat me," whimpered Little Gus. "I never even got to see Paris. . . ."

Just then the giant r'yari flopped across the rocks toward the thyss-cat. Quick as lightning, the huge beast pounced.

Little Gus and I got a gruesome preview of what might soon happen to us. The thyss-cat tore the r'yari to bits and gulped down the meat. In a matter of seconds, nothing was left of it but a spatter of purple blood on the rocks.

"Maybe it's full now," said Little Gus hopefully. The thyss-cat turned back toward him. It did not look full.

One pounce now, and it could cover the distance between it and Little Gus. I was paralyzed with fear.

"Run," I whispered.

Little Gus turned on his heels. In a flash, the thyss-cat hunched down like a coiled spring, then sprang high into the air. It was going to land right on top of him and bury its claws in his back. But just at the peak of its jump—a flying blur slammed into it!

"Get away from him, you ugly, six-legged son of a b—ch!" cried Hollins as he sailed through the air, kicking the beast aside. He was clinging to the rope—the other end was tied to a stalagmite at the top of the waterfall. By swinging down just in the nick of time, he'd saved Gus!

The thyss-cat rolled away but was back on its feet in an instant.

Hollins let go of the rope and landed on the shore. He pulled the folding knife from his belt and flicked it open. Now he stood between the thyss-cat and Little Gus. The beast still hadn't seen me.

"I'll hold it off!" he yelled to Little Gus. "You climb back up!" Gus grabbed the rope and started to scramble back up the rocks to the top of the waterfall. Nicki and Becky began to pull the rope at the top, hauling him up.

The thyss-cat roared and then charged at Hollins. He

dodged sideways and swung the knife. The cat yelped in pain and scrambled backward, a trickle of blood across its muzzle.

The cat was circling him now. Hollins had surprised it twice, and it seemed to be showing some caution. But in a long fight, it had every advantage. It was bigger, faster, and stronger than him. The folding knife looked awfully small compared with its fangs and claws.

The thyss-cat swiped again, catching Hollins across the leg. He grunted in pain. Now he was dripping blood too, from five wicked claw marks.

"Keep climbing," yelled Hollins through gritted teeth. Little Gus was nearly halfway up the rocks, his feet kicking wildly.

The thyss-cat leaped at Hollins, barreling him backward. Hollins fell down, and I saw the knife clatter away across the rocks and into the water. The cat was on top of him now, pinning him to the ground. He screamed.

If I didn't do something, Hollins was going to die. I started to run. The thyss-cat reared back to deliver the killing bite.

"Six legs son to the *b—ch!*" I screamed. I was paraphrasing Hollins—fear had temporarily garbled my human language skills.

I discharged my stink-gland right into the thyss-cat's

face. For an instant it was stunned, blinking and shaking its head and snorting. Its predator's sense of smell was many times more powerful than that of a Xotonian. Such a concentrated dose of stink must have been painful.

Then the thyss-cat whirled on me. I flipped backward, narrowly avoiding a deadly swipe to the face.

I was running for my life now. The thyss-cat was right behind me, water streaming from its yellow eyes. Ahead of me was a pile of fallen rocks. I started to scramble up it. But I knew there was no way I could climb fast enough.

The thyss-cat jumped and landed on my back, crushing me into the rocks. And then, to my surprise—the rocks gave way! Somehow we both fell right through them.

Now we were tumbling, end over end. Spinning down into darkness in a hail of loose stones. The thyss-cat clawed at me as we fell, until suddenly—it wasn't there anymore. I hit something hard, and I heard the cat scream, a sound that faded down into the distance until it was nothing at all.

All was dark. All was quiet. Was I dead? Killed by a thyss-cat while trying to save a human? Had I passed to the Nebula Beyond, where I would meet Great Jalasu Jhuk of the Stars and the other Xotonian ancestors?

After what seemed like an eternity, there came a distant voice.

"Chorkle," it said.

I saw a bright light.

"Chorkle!"

The light grew brighter.

I sat up, painfully. I was on the landing of a narrow stone staircase, clearly of Xotonian construction. On either side of the staircase was a sheer drop-off into darkness. I couldn't even see the bottom, it was so far below.

The light floated down toward me.

"Are you all right?" the light asked. But it was speaking a language that was not my own.

"Yes," I answered in human.

"Thank God," said Hollins as he put down his flashlight. He was covered in scratches, and he'd tied a makeshift bandage around the wound on his leg. "That's two human lives you saved today. Little Gus and I owe you."

"How badly are you hurt?" I asked.

"Not so bad," he said, rubbing his leg.

My mind began to form a fuzzy idea of what had just happened. The stairs back up—the direction from which Hollins had come—must lead to the rocky slope near the waterfall. The thyss-cat had somehow knocked me through an entrance to this chamber—an entrance that had been covered by a rockslide long ago.

"I think that that . . . animal went over the edge," said Hollins, shining his light downward into the darkness.

"Thyss-cat," I said.

Three more lights were coming down the stairs now: the other humans.

"Are you two dead or not?" said Becky. I could hear genuine fear in her voice.

"Sorry to disappoint you, Becky, but no," said Hollins.

"Idiots," Nicki said quietly. Then she put down her light and hugged Hollins, then me. Becky beamed.

Little Gus came last, trailing behind the girls. His face was turned downward, as though studying every inch of the stone staircase.

"Hollins . . . Chorkle, I, uh . . . I just wanted to say that . . . that I'm really sorry," he whispered. I could see that he was crying. "I almost got you two killed. . . ."

"It's okay. I've never seen a thyss-cat up close before. It was very impressive!" I said, trying to make him feel better. "Plus I almost killed you when I caused your pod to crash. So now the score is one to one."

"It's not a competition," sighed Becky.

"Anyway, I'm just really, really sorry . . ." said Little Gus, trailing off.

"Don't be sorry," snapped Hollins. "Just don't let it

happen again!" He was still angry, and understandably so. He had suffered a serious injury and come the closest to death of anyone in the fight.

"Don't let what happen again?" asked Nicki at last. "Getting towed over a waterfall by a big brain-fish?"

"Yeah," said Hollins.

"What about, say, two medium-sized brain-fish?" asked Becky.

"In that case . . . I guess . . . use your best judgment," said Hollins. And he started laughing despite himself. So did Nicki and Becky. Even Little Gus smiled, though tears still glistened in his eyes.

"We should get back to camp," said Hollins. "We've still got a mess of five medium-sized brain-fish to eat for dinner."

"Wait," I said, "I think—I think this place might be important."

"Where exactly are we?" asked Nicki, looking around.

"I don't know," I said. Despite the close proximity to the underground stream—I realized that we must actually be under the level of it now—these stairs were dry. Unlike the ruins nearby, the construction here was totally intact. This strange chamber must have dated back to ancient times. But for the thick layer of dust that covered everything, it looked as though it could have been carved yesterday.

How long ago had it been sealed off from the rest of the caverns?

"I think we need to go down," I said. The humans looked at one another.

"You good to walk?" Becky asked Hollins.

"I'm fine," he said.

"If you need help, you can, um, lean on me," said Nicki. "Only if you want to. You don't have to." But Hollins did.

The humans followed me, treading very carefully, since their safety rope was still tied to the stalagmite above. It was slow going with Hollins's wounded leg.

The strange staircase wound downward through the chamber with a landing every thirty meters or so, until at last it reached a wall. In the middle of the wall there was a door. It was made of solid iridium and had an eight-pointed star inset. Beside the door was a numerical keypad.

"An iridium door?" said Little Gus in a hushed tone. "Do you know how much that thing must be worth?" At least his sense of guilt over nearly getting everyone killed seemed to be fading fast. Little Gus's restless mind was sometimes a gift.

I stared at the keypad. On impulse, I punched in the same numerical combination that Kalac had used on the door of the Vault: 9-1-5-6-7-2-3-4.

The door slid downward with a rumble. Behind it stood a Xotonian, tall and handsome. It wore a strange military uniform and a fine green cloak, clasped with an eight-pointed star.

"Greetings," the Xotonian said, "I am Jalasu Jhuk."

CHAPTER NINETEEN

"**W**hat's it saying?" whispered Becky.

"Quiet!" I snapped, startling her.

It wasn't every day that you got to meet the quasi-mythical progenitor of your entire race. I was standing in front of *the* Jalasu Jhuk, hero of our oldest stories, the greatest Xotonian to ever live. The situation demanded some respect.

"I am most sorry, Great Jalasu Jhuk of the Stars," I said in formal Xotonian. "Please forgive my barbarous alien companions. They are but ignorant space hillbillies, unfit to touch the hem of your worst cloak."

But Jalasu Jhuk continued to speak over me, staring out into the middle distance.

"By now, I am gone," it said. "I left the entrance code to this chamber with a trusted few, with the instructions to open this door only if my plan failed. If you are here, listening to this message, then that likely means Gelo has been discovered and our enemies are coming for the Q-sik.

"If this is so, you must take it and flee to the Second Sanctum. The Q-sik is a weapon of unimaginable destruction, and not just for its intended target. Even at the lowest settings, the device can create a beam of energy powerful enough to tear a hole in the fabric of space-time. It is too dangerous to exist. Yet we cannot destroy it. Not yet, anyway.

"So you must do everything in your power to keep it from the Vorem and all others who would use it for conquest. Even those in the League. The fate of all beings in the universe—indeed, the fate of the very universe itself—hangs in the balance. You must not fail."

Then Jalasu Jhuk saluted, flickered, and disappeared.

"Jalasu Jhuk!" I cried. "Where did you go, O Great Progenitor?" Frantically, I looked around. But Jalasu Jhuk was nowhere to be found.

"It was a hologram," said Hollins.

My heart sank. Hollins was right. It had just been a three-dimensional projection from a tiny glass node on the wall. It was more lifelike than even the human hologram devices. Had Xotonians once been capable of creating such things?

"A hologram. Yes, of course," I said quietly.

I had looked upon Jalasu Jhuk with my own eyes. And for that, I considered myself unaccountably lucky. It was proof positive that our Great Progenitor was real, not just some legend. The message had mentioned the Vorem too. I could hardly believe it. It seemed that all Hudka's old stories were actually true. My mind reeled at the possibility.

But a great sadness welled up inside me too. It was profound to be so close to such a hero and yet so far away. Separated by countless years, separated by the barrier between life and death.

Such a pity it had been only a recording and not the real thing. We Xotonians could have used the guidance of a leader like our Great Progenitor in these troubled times. Perhaps Jalasu Jhuk would have known how to resolve our conflict with the human miners with honor and justice, without resorting to the Q-sik.

A cold feeling crept over me. The Q-sik. Despite Jalasu Jhuk's warning, we had already used it. Would this bring destruction to us, as Jhuk's message suggested? I wished I could just ask it. But Jhuk was long gone. And no one returns once they've passed to the Nebula Beyond.

"So who was that?" asked Little Gus.

"Great Jalasu Jhuk of the Stars," I said. "Someone very . . . very important to my people."

"And what did it say?" asked Becky.

"It said that we were welcome to enter the chamber," I lied. I hadn't mentioned the Q-sik to the humans yet, and I didn't intend to. It would likely mean answering a number of uncomfortable questions about the asteroid-quake that had stranded them here. Plus, the message from Jalasu Jhuk seemed to confirm that the ancient weapon should remain hidden from outsiders.

"The recording seemed to talk for an awfully long time just to say that," said Nicki delicately.

I said nothing as I stepped through the threshold to the chamber beyond.

It seemed to be constructed entirely out of iridium. The beams of the human flashlights bounced endlessly, reflecting off the silvery surface of every wall.

"Holy . . . crap," said Hollins, his eyes wide.

"There's more refined iridium in this one room than on the entire planet Earth," said Nicki.

"We're rich!" screamed Little Gus, overcome with excitement. "I'm gonna buy an ostrich and a new rocket-bike and the Tunstall 28x Holodrive, when it comes out, and an island! And then I'm going to hold a mysterious martial arts tournament on the island!" In his mind, he had just secured lifelong financial independence.

"Chorkle," said Nicki, looking around in awe. "Have you ever seen anything like this?"

I didn't answer. In fact, I hadn't. But the strangeness of an iridium room paled in comparison to what was inside it. Indeed, what I was looking at shocked me nearly as much as my face-to-face meeting with Jalasu Jhuk.

There, in the center of the chamber, sat three things that shouldn't exist. They were, unmistakably, Xotonian starships!

I bounded forward to get a closer look.

The ships were beautiful: sleek ellipsoids of glass and tarnished green metal. Each was big enough to hold a hand-ful of passengers and had a bulbous cockpit in the front and a swiveling blaster turret on top. These were serious ships; they looked like they could hold their own in a fight.

"So Xotonians do have starships, after all," said Hollins.

"We're not supposed to, but I—I guess we do," I said. "Or we did. It is said that long ago, our ancestors traveled the stars as easily as we walk between caverns today. But we all thought that was a myth."

"How much cash do you want for one of these ships, Chorkle?" asked Little Gus, now reckoning himself a very wealthy man in iridium. "I'll give you a million bucks."

"I'm not sure—"

"All right, a billion bucks!" said Little Gus. "You drive a hard bargain, my little alien friend."

"Maybe the ships aren't Chorkle's to sell," said Nicki.

"Can I at least rent one?" asked Little Gus. "I'd love to take one of these bad boys out for a spin. I'll be all, like, *vrooooooom*. 'Enemy ships detected, Captain!' 'Ready the lasers.' Pew! Pew, pew! Booooom!" He was now racing around, engaged in a fierce imaginary dogfight.

"I'd like to go on record as saying I don't think Little Gus should be operating any heavy machinery," said Becky.

"It does pose an interesting question," said Nicki, looking around. "Do you think they still work?"

"I don't know," I said.

"This place sure wasn't destroyed like the rest of the city up there," said Hollins. "Maybe the iridium kept the moisture and the mold out."

"Their systems might still be good to go," said Nicki.

"I bet you I could fly this thing," said Becky, wiping a layer of dust off the glass shield of the cockpit to get a look inside. "It's got a yoke and a throttle. Pretty much the same controls as the flight simulators we trained with before coming to this dumb asteroid—er, no offense, Chorkle."

"None taken," I said.

"Probably pretty similar to flying a rocket-bike, even,"

said Hollins, looking over her shoulder. "Except bigger and with more get-up-and-go."

"Too bad you don't know how to fly a rocket-bike," said Becky.

"Ha ha," said Hollins.

"If I push 'er any harder, captain, the whole thing's gaen to blow!" cried Little Gus to himself in strangely accented human. He now seemed to be losing the space battle against himself.

"Even if you could get the ships working, how would they get out of here?" asked Hollins. "We're deep inside the asteroid."

"I think I know," said Nicki, shining her flashlight on the ceiling of the chamber. There, high above, were hinges attached to heavy machinery. "This whole place opens." After she said it, it became clear what she meant: The ceiling was divided into two huge hinged sections that opened to the surface of Gelo. The biggest surface hatch ever. We were in a flight hangar large enough to hold many more ships than the three before us.

My mind was racing. The existence of these ships changed everything we knew about the Xotonian race. They meant that we were not just a pack of cave dwellers hiding on a little space rock called Gelo. We really had been the star-faring heroes that our legends promised!

But if Xotonians had made spaceships once, why did we no longer possess them? The ability to construct them—much less fly them—had been totally lost to us through the ages. Jalasu Jhuk said that the entrance code to the chamber had been kept a secret from most Xotonians of its own time. The location of this hangar, amid this ruined city, had apparently been forgotten. But why? Did Jalasu Jhuk itself have some reason for not wanting Xotonians to travel the stars?

"Let's see if we can open one up!" said Becky. "I want to sit in the cockpit for a minute. Just to get a feel for it."

We inspected the surface of one of the starships. On the side we found what seemed to be the entrance hatch. It was defined by a deep groove in the shape of a sinuous rectangle. And sure enough, beside it was a keypad.

I punched in the same code again: 9-1-5-6-7-2-3-4. Nothing happened. I tried again. Still nothing. I tried the keypads of the other two ships. I was out of luck. The code just didn't seem to work.

"Sorry," I said, shrugging. A sigh ran through the humans.

"Stand back, everybody," said Little Gus. "I got this." Then he wedged his fingers into the groove of the hatch and pulled as hard as he could. The hatch didn't budge.

"Ow," he said at last. And he walked away, flapping his hands in pain. It made sense that the seal, meant to stand up to the vacuum of space and the heat of atmospheric reentry, wasn't going to be broken by the strength of a tiny human boy.

"Hold on a sec," said Nicki, and she pulled out the Tunstall 24x Holodrive. "That keypad is electronic. After so long, it's possible that the ship's batteries simply ran down. Maybe I could give it just enough juice to bring it back online. A little jump-start, if you will. Then the ship might turn itself back on." She began to inspect the various technological inputs near the door. "I mean, I'm assuming they use computers to run. . . ."

"If we could bring one online," said Hollins, "then maybe we could fly it back to our parents!"

He was right. We might have just solved the problem of getting the young humans back to their own kind. It was a big "if," though.

"As long as I'm flying," said Becky, still gazing into the cockpit. "I don't trust anyone who got less than a ninety-seven percent pilot skill rating."

"Here we go!" said Nicki. She had found a small three-pronged hole in a panel by the door. "Anybody got, like, a pin?"

"Sis, please try not to shock yourself like you did with that ferroelectric capacitor you built for fifth-grade science fair," said Becky, handing her sister a small metal hairpin.

"Mild electrocution? Ha," Nicki was now muttering to herself. "I eat mild electrocution for breakfast."

She carefully bent the metal pin to convert the holo-drive's output cable from one prong to three.

"I'm curious, Becky," said Hollins. "What did you make for fifth-grade science fair?"

"Volcano," sighed Becky.

Nicki plugged in the cable and began typing code on the holodrive's virtual keyboard. She smiled.

"Good, I'm touching the ship's computer system. Luckily it's a solid-state drive. So first, we need to translate this ship's machine code into binary. This will take a few minutes," Nicki muttered to no one in particular. "Next, we translate it back into a programming language I know. Not perfect, but it gets it into semi-usable form. The executables to activate each of the separate systems should look pretty similar to one another. So if I can just figure out what one of those is, then maybe I can give it a little juice from the holodrive's battery. . . ."

After several minutes of furiously typing in silence, Nicki suddenly yelled, "Okay, here goes nothing!"

Indeed, nothing went. We waited. Nicki crinkled her nose.

"It's all right, Nicki," said Hollins, putting a hand on her shoulder. "Using a human computer to somehow inter-face with an ancient alien starship was never going to be—"

"Aha!" said Nicki, stopping deep in her code. "Syntax error. Forgot the semicolon at the end of line one hundred seventy-two. Let's try this again."

She did. And miraculously, the ancient starship lit up.

"It works!" cried Little Gus. Becky clapped Nicki on the back.

"Wow, you're a genius, Nicki," said Hollins.

"Yeah, you've got the glasses for a reason, sis!" said Becky.

"I wouldn't say it works quite yet," said Nicki, beam-ing. "I just brought the very simplest system back online: lighting. But to me it looks like the other systems should be functional. All except one. Really weird. It's got encryption like I've never seen before. But it's isolated. Doesn't seem necessary to the normal functions of the ship. Anyway, if you give me a few more hours, I guarantee you I could get the whole thing up and running. All three of them, even!"

"Great!" said Hollins, rubbing his injured leg. "After we get some food and sleep back at camp, we can come back first thing in the morning!"

"What? But I'm only eight, maybe nine percent done here!" cried Nicki. It ran contrary to her nature to walk away from an unsolved problem right in the middle of it. She wanted to stay and work on the starships. Little Gus wanted to stay too. He was nervous about leaving the iridium hangar unattended so that anyone could just steal it.

In the end, they relented and agreed to return after we'd eaten and rested. Together, we headed back up the winding staircase toward camp. It had been an eventful day; we were all tired and hungry.

At last, we climbed out the entrance onto the rocky shore beside the stream.

"Say, Chorkle," asked Little Gus above the roar of the waterfall. "How come you went all camo again?"

I looked down at my skin. It had again changed to the exact same shade as the rocks around us, an autonomic response to the threat of a nearby predator.

"Oh no," I said, my is'pog sinking. "Another thyss-cat!"

CHAPTER TWENTY

The group froze. Something inside me, some ancient tingle on the edge of awareness, had once again detected the presence of an ancestral predator. This reflex had turned my skin a dappled gray.

"Another thyss-cat?" groaned Becky. "Seriously? Two in one day? That's excessive."

"Maybe it's just a giant spider," I said hopefully as I scanned the rocks around us.

"And that's better . . . how?" asked Nicki.

"Everybody stick together," said Hollins, folding knife now in hand. "Don't get separated." He knew better than anyone just how dangerous a thyss-cat could be.

I swiveled all my eyes, scanning the spaces between the rocks for signs of the beast.

"There!" I cried, pointing about fifty meters down the

shore. I saw a patch of blue fur hunkered down between two boulders. The humans strained their eyes, but, as usual, they couldn't see that far.

Just then, we all heard a fearsome—meow?

"Huh. This one . . . doesn't sound quite as big," said Hollins.

We followed the sounds of mewling. Among the rocks we found a tiny thyss-cat. It was just a cub, only a few weeks old. Even I, the natural prey species of this animal, had to admit it was adorable. A little blue fur-ball with a pink tongue and huge yellow eyes. Its high-pitched distress squeaks pushed its lovability beyond all reason.

"Want hug," said Little Gus, reaching his arms out toward the cub. Apparently its cuteness level had garbled *his* human language skills.

"The big one was probably its mother," said Nicki, shaking her head. "Now she's . . ."

"We should—we should probably leave it here," said Hollins. But I could tell that even he wasn't immune to the little thyss-cub's charms.

"If we leave it, it will starve," I said. Immediately, Little Gus bent down to offer the cub a bit of dehydrated chicken cacciatore that he'd been keeping in his pocket. It sniffed at the strange reddish hunk. And then it sneezed.

"Awwww," we all said in unison. All except Becky, that is. Her judgment remained unclouded.

"Oh no," said Becky. "You all saw what happens when these things get bigger, right? Unstoppable killing machine. Remember? Nearly ate Hollins? This animal isn't nice."

"C'mon," said Little Gus. "If we hadn't—if I hadn't done what I did, its mom would still be alive right now." He was right. Although, I'd almost been killed and eaten by its mother, so I had a bit of trouble empathizing.

"I don't know," said Hollins. "Look at its little feet. They're like baby mittens."

"Six baby mittens," said Nicki softly as she bent down to rub the cub's left middle paw with her fingers. It squeaked.

"You've all lost your minds," cried Becky. "That's it! I'm assuming command here. Executive order: No alien kill-beasts as pets!"

"Please," said Little Gus. "It will be my responsibility. I'll clean up after it."

"What? Dude, we're not even talking about that! Look, when our parents come back for us, there's no way they're letting you bring that thing with you," said Becky. "You can't even take a pineapple through customs at the airport. You think you're going to get a space puma back to Earth?"

"Reeeeeowr," said the baby thyss-cat, suddenly and adorably.

"Did you hear that?!" cried Little Gus. "It just said 'Little Gus'! Everyone heard that, right?" Everyone nodded except Becky.

"Hopeless!" cried Becky, and she stalked off toward the rope, still dangling by the waterfall.

"Becky stopped arguing," said Little Gus.

"Never happened before," said Nicki. "I guess that means you won?"

"So I can keep it!" he cried.

"For now," said Hollins.

"My new best friend!" said Little Gus, and he reached down to pick up the cub. "Sorry, Chorkle, you just got bumped to the number-two slot. You should have been cuter."

"It's okay," I said, shrugging. I was secure enough to admit that the thyss-cub was significantly cuter than me.

"So what should I call the little monster?" he asked, stroking the cub's fuzzy chin.

"Manitou," said Hollins.

"Eigenket," said Nicki.

"Our Future Murderer," shouted Becky back toward us. She was already halfway up the rope.

"'Zhyddmor' means 'hunter' in Xotonian," I offered.

Little Gus nodded thoughtfully at all our suggestions. "Hmmm. I think I'm gonna name it . . . Pizza!" he said.

"Pizza?" asked Nicki, crinkling her nose. "Why?"

"Because. I. Love. Pizza!" he cried, and he lifted the thyss-cat cub above his head in triumph. Now and forever, the beast would be known as "Pizza."

"This is way better than an ostrich," said Little Gus, cuddling Pizza close to his chest as he walked back toward the dangling rope.

Nicki turned to Hollins. "You know, Becky's probably right. It probably isn't safe to let him keep it," she said quietly.

"I know," said Hollins. "But I think he needs this. Gus has had a rough couple of days. We all have."

Nicki nodded, and Hollins turned and limped toward the rope.

CHAPTER TWENTY-ONE

"**A**nd then the guy from the phone company was like, 'I'm sorry, miss . . .'" said Becky, pausing dramatically. "'But we traced that phone call . . . and it's coming from inside your own house!'" Becky leaned back. The light of the campfire danced on her face, turning her eyes into wells of deep shadow.

This was apparently the end of her story. None of the other humans seemed impressed.

"Nobody has land lines anymore," said Hollins.

"A few people still do," said Becky. "Anyway, this story happened a long time ago. When everyone had a land line."

"If you call your own phone number, don't you just get a busy signal?" asked Nicki.

"Not back then," said Becky.

"What happened after the phone-company guy traced the call?" asked Little Gus.

"Uh, the girl got out of the house just in the nick of time," said Becky. "That's what I heard."

"So no harm done," said Little Gus.

"No, the whole thing scared her very badly," said Becky. "Imagine getting a bunch of really spooky, threatening calls. In fact, those calls scared her so badly that—that she died."

"How does that work?" asked Hollins.

"Heart attack."

"You're telling us that a healthy teenage girl died of a heart attack?" asked Nicki. She sounded highly skeptical.

"Yeah. I mean, maybe she had, like, a condition before that . . ." Becky trailed off.

"And why did the mysterious caller do all this?" I asked.

"Oh, come on. Not you too, Chorkle," she said, sighing. "Look, I don't know. Maybe the dude was just crazy. I'm tired of answering questions. Someone else can tell a story, and I'll fact-check it." Becky scowled and crossed her arms.

We had all just eaten a meal of fried r'yaris—all five that Becky had caught earlier. After a brief, informal ceremony in which Becky was declared to be the winner of the contest with Hollins, Little Gus tossed them into the pan with a sizzle.

His culinary skills were evidently improving. He did a surprisingly good job of cooking them. He'd used salt, pepper, and just a hint of "synthetic lemon juice–like substitute." Everyone enjoyed the meal, even as they tried to forget that they were stuffing themselves with "brains that can swim."

"From now on, can we just refer to these things as 'tilapia'?" Hollins had asked as he chewed (apparently this was an aquatic species on Earth). All the humans agreed that a little wishful thinking would improve the experience.

Now we sat by the campfire in the philiddra forest, four human stomachs and one Xotonian z'iuk full of food. Pizza was snoring peacefully on Little Gus's chest. Even the thyss-cub had eaten its fill.

Apparently, proximity to an open fire will inspire a group of young humans to start telling what they call "ghost stories." Generally, these are implausible legends hinging on some morbid surprise or twist ending. Often, like the story of the mysterious caller, they involve no ghosts at all. And each of them seemed to know a few.

"Have you guys heard the story of the haunted minifridge?" asked Little Gus.

"Ugh," groaned Hollins. "Everyone's heard that story. And everyone knows it didn't happen."

"Did too!" said Little Gus. "My uncle's tax lawyer knew a guy who once saw the mini-fridge. And, friends, I don't want to scare you, but . . . it was still covered in green ectoplasm!"

"That was probably just rotten hummus," said Nicki. "And I'm sure the so-called groaning noises were caused by the buildup of gases inside airtight food containers."

"No way! They were the restless souls of all the victims the mini-fridge had claimed!" protested Little Gus.

"And you people thought my story was dumb," said Becky.

"Jeez, okay. I guess nobody wants to hear about the haunted mini-fridge," said Little Gus. "Every time you put yourself out there, it's a risk, Pizza," he said to the thyss-cub, who—as far as I could tell—was still asleep.

"There is one story I would like to hear," I said.

"What story is that?" asked Hollins.

"I would like to know how four young humans came to live on an asteroid far from their own blue-and-green world."

"Booo-ring," said Little Gus in a singsong tone.

"Well, I don't know if it's boring," said Hollins, scratching his chin. "Its not very scary, though. At least not until we were confronted by a strange alien being and we nearly suffocated to death. Meaning the parts you already know, Chorkle. Still want to hear it?"

"Totes," I said, trying out a little human slang.

"Well, I guess our story starts back on Earth, with something we call a 'multinational mining company.' Specifically, the Nolan-Amaral Corporation. See, for a long time, we've known that asteroids contain certain elements that are especially rare on our own planet."

"Like iridium," I said.

"Yup. Platinum too. And because of their rarity, these metals are very valuable to us. Extracting them from the crust of the Earth is Nolan-Amaral's whole business, worth billions of dollars a year. But not too long ago, the company decided it would be feasible—and profitable—to launch a manned mining mission to space.

"So they spent a few years building a spaceship and scoping out asteroids to mine. Eventually, they found one that seemed to fit the bill. A C-type asteroid with the exciting name of 48172-Rybar."

"Gelo," I said.

Hollins nodded.

"Why is this asteroid perfect?" I asked.

Here Nicki cut in. "Well, first off, 48172—er, Gelo, has ample iridium and platinum. That's the most important thing to a mining company. Gelo is big for an asteroid, over eight hundred kilometers in diameter. Big enough that you could call it a planetoid, even. And it has a super-dense core that gives it a similar gravity to Earth's. That means that a lot of Nolan-Amaral's existing mining equipment would need only minor modifications to work here."

"Anyway, the company pulled together a crew of experts," said Hollins. "They recruited my mom to be the commander of the whole mission. She's an astronaut. And they got my dad involved too, because he's an aeronautics engineer."

"Both of our parents are geologists," said Becky.

"And my pop does something with computers, I think," said Little Gus.

"His father is one of the foremost computer scientists on our whole planet," sighed Nicki. "He developed the Zaleski Theory of Artificial Intelligence."

"Zaleski? Hey, that's my last name. Cool," said Little Gus, thoroughly distracted by playing with the newly awakened Pizza.

"And are all of you also experts in some field?" I asked. The humans all looked at one another.

"Well, I hope to be a scientist one day," said Nicki. "Either biology or computer science, like Gus's dad. But I've got to finish middle school first. . . ."

"Becky won the World Arguing Championship three years running," said Hollins.

"Ha ha," said Becky. "No, we're not highly qualified like our parents. Not yet, anyway. We're just kids. The fact is, we're mostly here as a publicity stunt."

"Hey, c'mon," said Hollins. "That's not fair."

"Oh, you know it's true, Hollins," said Becky. "You see, Chorkle, Nolan-Amaral doesn't exactly have the best reputation back on Earth. The company is as famous for cutting down rain forests and propping up Third World dictators as it is for mining. So when they decided to undertake the mission, they thought up an angle that they could really sell to the public: kids in space."

"A less cynical interpretation would be that Nolan-Amaral didn't want to separate a bunch of parents from their children for a whole year," said Hollins.

"So you didn't have a choice?" I asked.

"I think we had a choice," said Hollins. "I wanted to come."

"Me too," said Nicki. "I figured there would be a lot to learn up here. And I wasn't wrong." She held up a plastic zip bag containing a withered fungal sample.

"I could've stayed with my uncle in New Mexico," said Little Gus, "but his whole house smells weird. Kinda like cabbage. So I came to space instead."

"I just thought it meant we would get to skip a year of

school," said Becky. "Little did I know that these sadists would prerecord fifteen hundred hours of the seventh grade and force me to watch every single day. And that's on top of all the astronaut training we had to do."

"I barfed in the centrifuge," said Little Gus.

"The training wasn't half as bad as going on all those talk shows," shuddered Nicki.

"I barfed on the set of *Good Morning, Ottawa*," said Little Gus.

"What's a talk show?" I asked.

"Well," said Hollins, "it's this thing where two people—a host and a guest—talk to each other. And this happens in front of a lot of other people who don't talk. But sometimes these other people clap ... Wow, when you think about talk shows, they're really weird."

"The talk show circuit was simply exhausting," said Becky.

Nicki snorted loudly with laughter. "Oh please, sis," she said. "You couldn't get enough media attention! You even framed the cover of that awful tabloid because they said the dress you wore to the Kids Boom! Awards was a 'fashion yes.'"

"Well, I'm not the one who tried to date celebrities," said Becky, grinning.

"That wasn't a date!" said Nicki sharply.

"It wasn't a date," said Hollins.

"Young Hollins here was seen by paparazzi getting ice cream with teen pop sensation Eryss," said Becky. I didn't know what "paparazzi" or a "teen pop sensation" were, but before I could ask, Hollins had to respond to the allegations.

"It was just some dumb thing her publicist set up with Nolan-Amaral," he said sheepishly. "She contacted me through Joynyt.com—sorry, Chorkle, that's a social networking site on Earth."

"What is a social networking site?" I asked.

"It's a virtual space where people post messages about themselves—and their cats—to other people," said Nicki. I nodded. I had no idea what she was talking about.

"Anyway," said Hollins, "yes, I got an ice cream with Eryss. No, it wasn't a date. She wasn't even nice."

"Was it a Feeney's Original Astronaut Ice Cream?" I asked.

"Wow, you really know how to cut to the heart of a story," said Little Gus.

"Chorkle, I think you've got astronaut ice cream on the brain," said Hollins. "I'm worried about you. I think you're addicted."

"Yeah," said Becky. "This is an intervention. We're cutting you off."

"Sorry, I already ate them all," I said. I was lying. I was still hoarding a box and a half. But I certainly did intend to eat them all.

"Anyway, that's the story of how we came to be here with our parents," said Nicki. "In retrospect, it kind of seems like a really terrible idea."

"Yeah," said Becky. "Kids in space isn't such good publicity if the kids get marooned on an asteroid and die."

"Hey!" said Hollins. "Our parents are coming back. Nobody's going to die."

His last word hung in the air. The group fell quiet, each of us lost in our own thoughts.

Even if these young humans eventually made it back to their parents, would they be able to explain that Xotonians weren't hostile? Would the humans even care? In fact, we'd already attacked their colony indirectly. And they were coming back with soldiers. If our two species did fight a war, then surely some people—human and Xotonian—*would* die.

Hollins sensed that the mood of the group had changed. As usual, he took it upon himself to try to boost everyone's morale.

"Hey, Gus," he said, "how about you tell us the story of that haunted freezer?"

"Haunted mini-fridge," Little Gus corrected him. "Well, it all started with a strange scratching noise coming from the vegetable crisper—"

"Wait," said Becky, "did anyone else just hear something?"

"C'mon. Stop trying to scare everyone," said Nicki.

"No, really! Be quiet. Listen."

We were silent. Each pop and crackle of the fire was now amplified to the volume of a footfall. And the strange shadows of the gnarled philiddra forest seemed to push in against the light. I couldn't stop thinking about the Xotonian skull I'd found buried in the dirt before.

"I don't hear anything," said Hollins at last.

"Yeah," said Becky, "I guess I was just imagining—"

Crunch. We all heard it this time. The sound of something—or someone—away in the distance, moving through the forest. Another crunch. We stared at one another. Whatever it was, it was coming toward us.

CHAPTER TWENTY-TWO

I checked the color of my skin. Its shade was unchanged. At least it wasn't yet another thyss-cat.

"Everybody down. Put out that fire," said Hollins quietly. All four of the humans dropped to the ground. Becky threw a cup of water on the fire, and it died with a hiss. Now the embers were just a bloody red glow.

"You see anything, Chorkle?" whispered Hollins.

With the fire out, my eyes could pierce further into the darkness. I saw something creeping through the mist, moving between the trunks of two philiddra. Then I saw another. And another. Several figures were converging on our campsite.

"Yes," I whispered. "Four or five. They're coming for us."

"Four or five? Four or five what?" whispered Little Gus. "I thought you said nobody lives here!"

"Nobody does," I said. But I wasn't so sure anymore. I could see the shape of the figures more clearly now. The silhouettes were Xotonian.

We were camping in the overgrown ruins of what had once been a second Xotonian city. Did some lost remnant of those ancient Xotonians still inhabit this wilderness? Had we trespassed in their caverns and angered a wild, long-forgotten clan of my species?

Worse yet, maybe there weren't any Xotonians still living here. Maybe these moving shadows were the spirits of the restless dead, stuck on this side of the Nebula Beyond, angry that we had disturbed the silence of their forgotten funeral city. Maybe, as Little Gus worried, there were indeed ghosts in this place.

"I think," I said quietly, "we need to run."

The young humans leaped to their feet, and together we raced through the forest, headed in the opposite direction of the approaching Xotonians. Their flashlights swung in the darkness as they ran.

Even with his hurt leg, Hollins took the lead. But it was hard for the humans to see where they were going. The terrain was slick and uneven, and the branches of the philiddra whipped at their arms and faces.

I could hear our pursuers close behind us now. As I said

before, Xotonians are thoroughly suited to moving through the shadowy caverns we inhabit. It was no surprise that they were gaining on us.

From the corner of my fourth eye, I saw Nicki fall. She was tangled up in something. A net?

"Go on!" she screamed.

At this, Hollins turned his head back to look for her. Right then, a Xotonian jumped out from behind a philiddra trunk in front of him.

"Ver'sald!" it cried, the Xotonian word for "stop."

Hollins didn't understand, and he wouldn't have obeyed if he had. Instead he whipped up his flashlight, shining its beam right into the Xotonian's face. It screamed and cringed at the pain of such bright light in its eyes. In that instant, Hollins dove at it, knocking it right off its fel'grazes. The two of them struggled in the mud, turning over and over.

Nearby, Becky had been cornered by another Xotonian, her back against a boulder. I could see a blaster clutched in its thol'graz.

"What do we do?" asked Little Gus. He was beside me, clutching Pizza, who yowled pitifully the whole time.

"Up here," I said, and I grabbed him by the arm. Then I began to climb the trunk of a huge, ancient philiddra, carrying him up with me.

I looked back toward Becky as I climbed. She was holding both her hands up in surrender now. The Xotonian had its blaster trained on her. Then, all of a sudden, she lunged and punched it hard, right in the z'iuk. The blaster fell from its grasp. Somehow Becky managed to kick it away.

"Oh crap," said Little Gus. "They saw us!"

Down below us another Xotonian had started to climb the trunk of our philiddra. Little Gus wasn't big as far as humans go, but he was about the same size as me. Carrying his added weight made it twice as difficult to pull myself up through the branches, and I soon felt a burning pain in my muscles.

Near the top, I yanked Little Gus with me out onto a thick branch. Our Xotonian pursuer climbed quickly. It too was holding a blaster.

Gus and I backed away from the trunk. The further out we got on the branch, the thinner it became. Now it swayed dangerously with every movement, and Little Gus was having trouble keeping his balance. There was nowhere to go now but down, I realized.

Below, I saw Becky. She lay on the cavern floor, tangled in a net. Two Xotonians stood over her.

But then there was Hollins running toward them. He was holding something in his hands and pointing it at them.

A blaster! He must have somehow grabbed the one that Becky had kicked away! One of the Xotonians pointed its own blaster right back at him—a standoff.

Meanwhile, our Xotonian was stepping out onto our branch now. The added weight shook it violently.

"No!" cried Little Gus. And he slipped from the branch and fell. My thol'graz darted out, and I managed to catch hold of him. But his weight swung me around to the bottom of the branch. Now I was hanging on to the branch for my life. Little Gus was clinging to me and holding Pizza in his other hand.

The Xotonian crept closer. There was something familiar about this one.

"Chorkle," said Kalac as it recognized me, "what have you done?"

CHAPTER TWENTY-THREE

We marched along in silence. Six Xotonians and four humans. The humans were tied together again. This was not for safety. They were prisoners now.

Kalac led the Xotonian group, a group that included Sheln and three other able-bodied warriors.

A scout had found human footprints near the Jehe Canyon surface entrance and reported back to the Chief of the Council. They had tracked us through the Unclaimed Tunnels for over three days.

"I—I thought that I was helping them," I said to Kalac as we walked. "I just didn't want them to get hurt. . . ."

Kalac said nothing. My originator had not spoken to me since the humans had agreed to surrender.

Becky, Nicki, and Little Gus had all been captured back in the philiddra forest. But Hollins and one of the other

Xotonian warriors—Eromu was its name, an officer of the city guard—had held each other at blaster-point. Both of them were ready to shoot.

"Tell that thing to let us go," Hollins had said.

"I don't think that's possible," I said. "I'm sorry, Hollins." I had tried to keep the young humans away from other Xotonians. I had failed.

"You can understand these fur-headed creatures?" said Kalac to me, in our own language. Astonishment momentarily exceeded my originator's anger.

"Yes, I can," I said. I suddenly felt ashamed, like it was somehow wrong to have learned the language of the invaders.

"Then you tell this human that I will blast it to pieces," growled Eromu, gripping its blaster. "Even if it kills me too. I don't fear the Nebula Beyond!"

"Chorkle, you know us," said Hollins. "Just tell them we mean them no harm!"

Sheln and the other two warriors, Ornim and Chayl, now had their blasters trained on Hollins as well. There was a glee in Sheln's eyes. I knew it would love nothing more than to vaporize a real-life human.

"Put the blaster down, Hollins," I said in his language. "I don't want anyone to get hurt. If you surrender, I promise no harm will come to you. If you don't, I think—I think you'll die."

Hollins gritted his teeth and squeezed the handle of the blaster. For a moment, he looked like he meant to go out in a fiery blaze.

"I thought you were on our side," he said at last. And he dropped the weapon.

"I'm sorry," I said. But Hollins wouldn't look at me.

Now we marched back toward Core-of-Rock. Kalac led us by a different route than the way I had brought the humans. It was much shorter and more direct. Apparently, the lost second settlement was not so far from my home city after all. And Kalac had known of the place's existence all along.

I wanted to ask Kalac about those blackened ruins, to tell my originator that we had found starships—actual Xotonian starships! But I kept quiet. Even if Kalac had been speaking to me, I was terrified that the ships could be used to attack the rest of the humans. That would guarantee an all-out war.

I looked back. The young humans walked single file, tied at the wrists with their own rope. In each of their faces I saw something different. Hollins was defiant. Becky was furious. Nicki looked nervous. And Little Gus had tears glistening in his eyes. I hadn't spoken with them since the surrender either. I felt like I'd betrayed them.

In all the confusion, I'd managed to stuff Pizza in an empty box of Feeney's Original. So far, the thyss-cub had been smart enough to stay quiet. Like humans, thyss-cats—even the young ones—were feared and despised by most Xotonians. Every so often I'd crack the lid of the box slightly and see the cub's bright yellow eyes shining back at me.

As usual, a journey through the winding tunnels of Gelo was hard for the humans. None of them dared ask for a rest, though. Either they were too afraid of their captors or they didn't want to show weakness. Hollins was limping heavily on his injured leg. Behind him, Little Gus stumbled.

"We need to stop," I said. "Humans can't walk as far as we can underground. They need rest."

Without a word to me, Kalac held up its thol'graz as a signal to the others. The group stopped.

Little Gus nearly collapsed in exhaustion on the floor of the tunnel. Nicki and Becky sat down and began to whisper quietly among themselves. Hollins remained standing. His fists were balled.

Eromu, Ornim, and Chayl watched the humans as though they were the deadliest creatures in the universe. It was much the same way the young humans had regarded me at first.

I approached them. Eromu glared at me like I was a traitor. Maybe I was? I wasn't so sure anymore.

"Here," I said to Nicki. And I handed her four Feeney's Original Astronaut Ice Cream bars.

"Thanks, Chorkle," she said quietly. She took one and passed the rest to the others. Hollins shook his head. Nicki handed his bar back to me.

"What are you saying?" Sheln yelled. "Stop speaking human to them!"

"Mind your own business!" I yelled back. "I didn't do anything wrong!" My outburst startled Sheln. Even I was a little surprised at the volume of my voice. A few weeks ago, I couldn't have imagined myself shouting down a member of the Council—or any other elder, for that matter.

"Yes, you did," said Kalac quietly. My originator had decided to speak to me at last. "You did do something wrong. You ruined our plan. If you had done nothing, our world would be safe from the invaders right now. Instead you sneaked aboard their vessel. For some reason beyond all knowing, you sneaked aboard. And they saw you. They saw you, Chorkle! We were monitoring the humans' transmissions the whole time. Now they know that there are

Xotonians on Gelo. Even worse, we've abducted four of their offspring—Jalasu Jhuk, help us. The humans are sure to come looking for them."

I wanted to respond, but everything my originator had just said was true. The situation was worse, perhaps, than even Kalac knew.

"What? Nothing to say?" said Kalac.

"I tried to do the right thing," I said.

"In trying to do the right thing, you have doomed us all," said Kalac. Its voice was as hurt and disappointed as I'd ever heard it sound. "I'm sorry I ever originated you."

And Kalac turned and began to walk again.

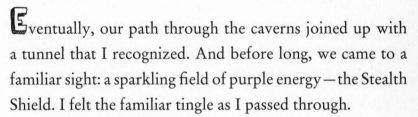

CHAPTER TWENTY-FOUR

Eventually, our path through the caverns joined up with a tunnel that I recognized. And before long, we came to a familiar sight: a sparkling field of purple energy—the Stealth Shield. I felt the familiar tingle as I passed through.

The humans were cautious, reluctant to cross the shield. But Eromu yanked their rope, and one by one, they stumbled through. Even in her distress, I could tell that Nicki was fascinated, already trying to deduce the nature and purpose of the energy field.

We walked through the outskirts of Core-of-Rock. All the humans stared wide-eyed now—except Hollins. He kept up the same neutral expression he'd had the whole journey.

They stared at the fields of cultivated mushrooms, the domed Xotonian farmhouses and spiraled silos, the usk-lizards chewing their cud. Likewise, the rural Xotonians of these parts came out of their homes and stood beside the path to gape at the captured aliens.

"Looky there," I heard one originator whisper to its offspring. "Ain't got but two eyes apiece."

By this point, the humans had only seen the Unclaimed Tunnels (which were impressive in their own wild way). But now they looked upon the twinkling lights of a complete underground society. We passed merchants and stonemasons and guards patrolling atop big usk-lizards (all of whom froze in their tracks when they saw four humans walking by). We saw bridges and canals and spires climbing toward the roof of the massive chamber. Core-of-Rock was a bustling subterranean community, quite unlike anything on all of Eo.

If we had been visiting under different circumstances, I could have played tour guide to the humans. I could have shown them Ryzz Plaza and the Great Geode and the Plebiscite Pool. I could take them to the market stall that had the absolute best stuffed cave slugs (Sertor's, of course). I could point out the unmarked trash dump where Linod had collected several of its most fascinating "fascinating fungi." Nicki, if no one else, would enjoy that.

But there was no happiness in this visit. I looked back

and saw four travel-worn young humans. They were captives on an alien world, and they were terrified—no matter how much they tried to conceal it. For all they knew, they were marching to their doom in this dark underground city.

"Chorkle!" cried a familiar voice. Hudka stood by the street up ahead, amid a small crowd of Xotonian onlookers. It was leaning heavily on its gnarled cane. Somehow it looked even older and more fragile than when I'd seen it last.

"Hudka!" I cried, and I ran and hugged my little grand-originator.

"I was worried about you, kid. But I figured you're smart enough to handle yourself," said Hudka.

"Not this time," I said to Hudka. "I tried to help, but it didn't work. I messed everything up."

"Eh, at least you tried. And if things always worked out," said Hudka, "just imagine how boring life would be."

The humans and the other Xotonians trudged past us now.

"My, my, you sure caught some dangerous humans," said Hudka to Kalac. "Mighty warriors, all of you." Kalac said nothing.

"Shut your gul'orp," muttered Sheln.

"That small one with the red head-fur looks like a real

killer, Sheln," said Hudka, pointing to Little Gus. "Maybe they'll put up a statue of you in Ryzz Plaza next. You brave hero, you."

At that, Sheln started toward Hudka, but Ornim and Chayl managed to hold it back. This seemed to be one of Sheln's all-time favorite moves: the old lunge-and-restraint.

"You just wait, you withered husk," said Sheln.

"Wait for what?" said Hudka. "I've been waiting. How much older do I have to get before whatever it is happens?"

"Stop it. Both of you," said Kalac.

"The Chief of the Council has spoken," said Hudka, bowing sarcastically. "C'mon, Chorkle. It's time to go home." Hudka put a thol'graz around me and started back toward our dwelling.

"No, Hudka," I said. "I'm sorry, but I can't go home yet. I'm not going to leave these humans. They're my responsibility."

As I said it, I turned to look Kalac right in the eyes. I was sure my originator expected me to cower at home in terror. To think on my sins at home for hours, until it returned later to mete out some righteous punishment, possibly dis-owning me. But I wasn't about to leave the humans alone with the likes of Sheln. Who knew what it had planned?

"Chorkle is right," said Kalac. "It is not going home. It

is coming with us." And it turned and continued walking. The rest of the group followed behind.

Chorkle is right. Kalac's words echoed in my mind. Somehow that was the most terrifying thing it could have said.

"Well, good luck, Chorkle," said Hudka. "I'll see you back at our place. You're gonna wish you never came back when you see my high score in Xenostryfe III."

"Hey, Hudka," I said, "can you take this box back to our house and keep it safely in my room?" I gave my grand-originator a knowing look and handed it the Feeney's box containing Pizza the thyss-cub.

Hudka took a quick look inside the box but didn't balk. It simply nodded and pushed its way past the group of onlookers, toward our home. As it walked away, I heard Pizza mewl loudly.

"Rild-sauce didn't agree with me," said Hudka to no one in particular as it rubbed its z'iuk. "Terrible, terrible gas." No one seemed interested in exploring the matter further.

By the time we reached the Hall of Wonok—the usual meeting place for the Council—a huge crowd had gathered outside it. Word of the alien parade had traveled fast. It was almost an impromptu Grand Conclave.

"Step aside," said Kalac. "Let us pass." Slowly, the crowd began to part.

"Invaders!" someone cried. "You mess with Xotonians and you see what happens."

"Human scum!" cried another.

"Oh, why won't they just leave us alone!" blubbered another.

"All of you need to calm down," said Kalac. "This isn't your concern. This is Council business."

"Isn't our concern? You brought a bunch of dirty space aliens into our city!" cried someone else. "What if they have Eo diseases?"

The hole in the crowd had closed behind us. We were completely surrounded now as we slowly moved toward the entrance to the hall.

"Ugh, look!" someone shrieked. "Two of them are exactly the same! It's unnatural!" The crowd jostled even closer, presumably for a better vantage point. The humans were frightened.

"Eromu, Ornim, Chayl," said Kalac firmly. "Keep these people back." The three warriors didn't look too eager to fight their own kind to protect a bunch of humans.

"We should kill those freaks," said someone, "before they kill us." There were cries of agreement.

I turned to face the crowd. "They're not dangerous!" I yelled. "They're only kids. Anybody who touches them is losing a thol'graz!" A hush fell over the mob. I had stunned everyone into temporary silence.

"Was that Chorkle?" I heard someone in the back whisper. Admittedly, shouting down an angry mob was a bit out of character for me.

We opened the huge, heavy door and passed into the Hall of Wonok. The Xotonian crowd pushed its way to the threshold, behind us.

"Eromu," said Kalac, "go find Loghoz, Glyac, and Dyves. Tell them to come here." Eromu nodded and pushed its way back out through the crowd.

"Bar the door and guard it," said Kalac to Ornim and Chayl. "Keep three eyes on that crowd. No one who isn't on the Council may pass." Ornim and Chayl nodded and then slowly swung the massive door shut, leaving the Xotonian mob outside.

The hall was a single large room, the seat of Xotonian government. At one end, an eight-sided podium faced a wide, black onyx table. Behind the table was enough terraced seating for a few hundred citizens. A speaker could stand at the podium and address the seated Council and the crowd assembled behind it. During the course of Kalac's political career, I'd been to more than a few Xotonian Council meetings—perhaps the universe's most effective cure for insomnia.

Attendance never neared capacity. Only a few dozen of Core-of-Rock's most eccentric ever turned out (Hudka, of course, was always among them).

Today there were none here but us. The emptiness caused sound to echo strangely around the room.

"Sit down," said Kalac, in Xotonian, to the humans. It indicated the first row of tiered seats. The humans looked at one another uncertainly.

"You can sit down," I said in human. All of them did, even Hollins. I approached the humans and began to untie the rope that bound their wrists.

"What in the name of Morool are you doing?" yelled Sheln.

"I'm sorry, Sheln," I said, continuing with the ropes. "I didn't realize you were so terrified of these baby humans. Don't look now, dude, but your shadow is right behind you." I threw in the human word "dude" purely because I thought it might vex Sheln even more (and I was right). Hudka was really on to something: Vexing Sheln was its own reward.

"What . . . don't you 'dude' me. . . . I'm not scared. . . . I'm—I'm street smart!" sputtered Sheln, and it looked to Kalac for some support. Kalac offered nothing.

"When the other three members arrive," said Kalac, "I

intend to convene a special closed meeting of the Xotonian Council."

"So why am I here?" I asked.

"Yeah," said Sheln, "why is that disrespectful little piece of —"

Kalac's icy glare managed to stop Sheln from saying something truly insulting about its offspring. "Why is young Chorkle still here?" it continued.

"For better or worse, Chorkle is the only one of us who speaks the human language," said Kalac. "We'll need a translator for the interrogation."

CHAPTER TWENTY-FIVE

"Tell . . . 'Sheln,' was it?" said Becky, squinting as she stood at the podium. "Tell Sheln that it looks exactly like a cross between a horseshoe crab and a pile of dirty diapers. Only fatter."

"You know I can't tell it that, Becky," I said, sighing.

"What is this one saying?" said Sheln. "Translate everything exactly as she says it, Chorkle! Despite your evident love of the invaders, you cannot editorialize! I heard my name. Did she threaten me?"

"She said that she wishes for peace between our two great peoples," I said to Sheln.

"The last time she used that exact phrase," squealed Dyves fearfully, "it sounded different."

"The human language is very complex," I said.

"Please, can we just contact our parents?" pleaded

Becky. "I'm sure a quick conversation could sort all this out."

It was not the first time the humans had asked this. Again, I translated. The Council conferred.

"The humans may not contact their originators," said Loghoz. "They could send secret messages or relay strategic information about Xotonian defenses. Please tell 'Beck-ee' that she is a prisoner and in no position to ask things of us. She is to answer our questions."

I relayed this to Beck-ee.

"We've already told them all we know," she said wearily. "There isn't any more! Does everyone here get that we're kids? Not high-value military targets. Kids don't know anything! If the Council wants my Joynyt.com password, they can have it. Otherwise, I'm not sure what else I can give them."

I translated. The Council conferred.

"The Council would like," said Loghoz at last, "her Joynyt.com password."

Becky sighed. Then I tried, in vain, to somehow translate "rocketchick0825" into Xotonian. If the Council were ever to gain access to something called "the Internet," Becky's personal profile might be mined for useful intelligence.

The humans had been answering questions for hours. All

except Hollins, who had refused to answer anything at all. When he was called, he stood at the podium respectfully but said nothing. He kept a neutral expression on his face, though sometimes I caught him glaring at me when he thought I wasn't looking. Evidently, he still blamed me for their capture.

To my knowledge, the other three had answered truthfully. No, the asteroid-mining mission was not a military invasion. Yes, their parents planned to return in three days to rescue them. No, humans did not possess blaster-weapon technology. Yes, Commander Hollins did say they were coming back with soldiers. No, Commander Hollins did not say how many soldiers. Yes, they did have a general awareness of the leadership structure of the Nolan-Amaral Corporation. No, they did not know who the current CEO was. And so on.

By now, their interrogators were just going in circles, repeating themselves and fixating on the insignificant. At one point the Council even forced Nicki to explain to them in great detail how internal combustion heat engines work and how these engines can be attached to a spacecraft to allow said spacecraft to achieve escape velocity for a planet's—or an asteroid's—gravitational field.

"So," Glyac had said, startling everyone by speaking for

the first time, "how quickly could you build one of these human spacecraft for us?" I translated.

"By myself?" said Nicki, doing some quick mental math. "Maybe seventy years? But I'd need all the parts in advance."

The Council wasn't getting the answers it wanted. And as time dragged on, nearly everyone—human and Xotonian alike—had become frustrated and irritable. Kalac and Hollins remained calm, however. My originator asked the occasional question but nothing more. Hollins kept his mouth shut.

"We're getting nowhere. The big one—'Hah-lens,' or however you say it—why won't he answer our inquiries?" sniffed Dyves, tears beginning to well in its eyes. This was approximately the fifteenth time the same question had been posed.

"As I said, he believes he's a prisoner of war. And under the 'Geneva Conventions,' he says he can refuse to answer your questions." I didn't fully understand his position myself, and I hadn't gotten it directly from Hollins. Nicki had tried to explain it to me at the beginning of the interrogation.

"So he's declaring war on us?" asked Loghoz.

"What?" snorted Glyac, suddenly waking up.

"No, he's not declaring war," I said.

"I think the big one's hiding something," said Dyves.

"I swear by Jalasu Jhuk that he's not!" I said. "The others have told you everything that he knows. You're just wasting your breath now."

"Chorkle may be right," said Sheln. "Perhaps there has been too much talking and not enough action. Maybe this big one, Hah-lens, needs a little . . . persuasion."

"What are you talking about?"

"Let me put it this way: I never agreed to anything called the 'Juh-nee-vuh Con-ven-shuns,'" said Sheln, mangling the human words. "So maybe a little pain would help this one to find his voice."

"You—you want to torture them?" I asked. I couldn't believe it. I turned to Kalac. My originator was silent, unreadable.

"Call it what you will," said Sheln. "If he won't speak, then maybe he'll scream. . . . All of them will."

"We've tried everything else," said Loghoz.

"I simply can't bear the thought of it," said Dyves. "But if we must, we must. . . ."

Glyac merely grunted in assent.

I looked to the humans now. The tenor of the Xotonian conversation had changed. They could tell something was different, and they were afraid.

"Chorkle, what are they saying?" asked Little Gus.

"What's going on?" said Becky.

Somehow I had known Sheln would try something like this. Its blind hatred of all humans was too great.

"I propose that we proceed with . . . harsher interrogation techniques," said Sheln. "All those on the Council in favor—"

"No!" I cried before anyone could raise a thol'graz. "You listen to me very carefully, Sheln. These humans are my responsibility. If you want to torture them, you have to get through me. I'll die before I let you hurt them."

"Kalac, your offspring is here to translate, not to—"

"I will put this situation in very simple terms," I said. "You have four human children, including the son of the commander of the mining expedition, here in your custody. If you deliver them safely to their parents, a war may be averted. If you harm them instead, I guarantee you that the rest of the humans will stop at nothing—nothing—to get their revenge. Just imagine how you would feel if you were in their position. If humans mistreated your offspring, Zenyk." I was shaking with anger now.

"So no," I said, "you will not torture them. Not while I'm still breathing."

"Then that makes you an enemy as well," cried Sheln.

"I say let the hoo-mins come! Let them try to invade our tunnels. We can hold them off forever. We have blasters! We have seventeen personal shields!"

"You almost sound like you want a war," I said.

"So what if I do?" cried Sheln. "Why shouldn't we crush them? Why shouldn't we prove our strength in fire and blood! We could be legends, like Jalasu Jhuk and the rest of them!"

Sheln was raving. The rest of the Council members were staring at it now.

"Why should Xotonians always have to hide?" said Sheln.

"Chorkle is right," said Kalac. "We do not torture. These young humans have nothing more to tell us. It's foolish to assume that they would know anything useful about human military operations."

Kalac was staring at me now. There was a hint of something in its eyes, something new.

"Tell the humans they may go," said my originator.

"But you can't do—wait, what?" I said.

"They are still prisoners, but they will not be harmed. They may move about freely within Core-of-Rock," said Kalac, "if they promise not to attempt escape."

"You can't be serious?" cried Sheln. But everyone ignored it.

I translated Kalac's offer to the humans. In turn, each of them nodded in agreement to the promise. Last came Hollins. He nodded too. He didn't look angry anymore.

"Hey, Chorkle," he said quietly, "I don't speak your language, but I'm pretty sure you just went to bat for us. Thanks."

I shrugged.

"The Council still has much to discuss and decide," said Kalac. "Chorkle, your translation services are no longer needed. Please take the humans and leave. They can stay at our dwelling for the time being."

"Thank you, Kal—er, Chief of the Council," I said. I recognized the look in Kalac's eyes now. It was respect.

"You were right on another point," said Kalac. "For better or worse: These humans are here because of you. They are your responsibility now."

CHAPTER TWENTY-SIX

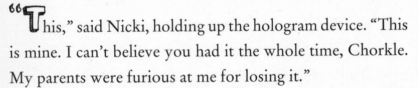

"This," said Nicki, holding up the hologram device. "This is mine. I can't believe you had it the whole time, Chorkle. My parents were furious at me for losing it."

"Sorry," I said. "When I, er, borrowed it, I still thought you were just a gross space alien."

Nicki scowled.

"That was a wonderful time," said Becky, clapping Nicki on the back. "Losing that Tunstall 24x Holodrive was the first thing Nicki has ever done wrong in her life. Took some of the heat off ol' Becky. Ma and Pa García got so mad they started yelling en español."

"What's español?" I asked.

"Spanish," said Becky. "It's the language that everybody speaks where our parents come from."

"Wait," I said, "you're telling me that there's more than

one human language?"

"There are approximately seven thousand human languages," said Nicki. My is'pog sank. So far, I'd felt rather proud of my human-ese fluency. Apparently, I still had a lot to learn.

We were together in my dwelling, the humans' temporary new home. They had been exhausted from their long march through the tunnels and the subsequent interrogation. Immediately after we had arrived, all of them had crashed. They had slept for hours, wherever they had sat or lain.

Kalac had not yet returned home. Apparently, the Council was still debating an appropriate course of action.

Now everyone was awake (it had taken all of us to rouse Becky) and rested. I whipped up a pretty standard Xotonian breakfast of rild-sauce over cold svur-noodles. The humans were polite, if not enthusiastic, about eating it.

Postbreakfast, we relaxed in the living chamber. Hudka observed us quietly from its chair in the corner.

"Chorkle, what are they talking about?" whispered Hudka as it watched Nicki handling the holodrive. "She doesn't want to take the hologram computer thingy back, does she? Tell her she can't have it! I'm so, so close to saving the princess that the reptile king abducted."

"I think we can keep it for now," I said.

"Yo, Chorkle, how old is Hudka anyway?" asked Little Gus as he played with Pizza on the floor. "It looks like a walking Craisin. No offense."

"I don't really know," I said. "A few hundred years?"

"What did that little red-furred one say?" said Hudka. "I heard 'Hudka.'"

I translated Little Gus's comment accurately. I even explained that—according to Nicki—"Craisin" was a proprietary (yet widely used) term for the dehydrated version of an Eo fruit known as a "cranberry."

"So he's saying I'm wrinkled?" said Hudka after absorbing all of this.

"Yeah, I think so," I said.

Hudka considered it for a while and then laughed suddenly, startling the humans. Again, Xotonian laughter is a loud metallic honking sound. And Hudka's laughter is louder than most.

"Tell him that his head-fur is the same color as a cave-ape's butt," said Hudka. I translated this into human.

"Then cave-apes must have beautiful, lustrous butts," said Little Gus. I translated this back into Xotonian. Hudka laughed again.

And so a friendship between Hudka and Little Gus was born. Though my grand-originator didn't speak much of their language—Hudka's "linguistic hyperaptitude" seemed to be a little less "hyper" than mine, perhaps due to advanced age—it certainly enjoyed human company. Most especially because it meant that, with two holodrives, we could now play our favorite games in four-player mode.

Hudka, Nicki, Little Gus, and I spent the morning blasting legions of virtual flying saucers. Little Gus wasn't as quick on the holographic draw as the rest of us, but he got particularly upset when he lost. And Hudka found this hilarious.

Another quirk of human video games: As fun as they are to play, they are exactly that boring to watch. Perhaps even more so. Becky and Hollins were mostly relegated to sitting around the house while the rest of us played. Soon they became restless.

"Say, Chorkle," said Hollins, standing and stretching, "what if we took a walk or something? I mean, Kalac said it was okay, and Kalac's in charge, right?"

"Yeah," said Becky, "I know you guys want to win the war on pixels, but I'm starting to lose my mind. Your asteroid really needs Internet."

"Oh really? That's very interesting," I said to Becky. I wasn't really listening. My focus lay squarely with the hologram game.

At last, Hollins and Becky dragged us from the holodrives, and we all prepared to venture out into the city.

"Hudka should come with us," said Little Gus. "I'm loving your 'grand-originator.' It's like one of those hairless cats for people with allergies. But it can talk."

I translated for Hudka.

"These kids want to go outside instead of playing video games?" said Hudka, shaking its head scornfully. "Life's too short for that." And my grand-originator switched Xeno-stryfe III to one-player mode.

Kalac had officially decreed that the humans were allowed to move around Core-of-Rock freely. Still, I worried about their safety. Wherever we went, they were bound to arouse curiosity, at best. At worst: outright hostility. I wasn't eager to confront another angry mob, as I had outside the Hall of Wonok.

My originator was Chief of the Council, and its word protected the humans. I just hoped that would be enough.

Pizza stayed behind with Hudka—I reckoned the city was even more dangerous for a thyss-cat than a human— and we walked out my front door and down the steps.

Sure enough, about a dozen Xotonians were milling around outside, all trying to look casual. By now, everyone in Core-of-Rock must have known that this is where the humans were staying.

"We come in peace," said Hollins, holding one hand up.

"Very original," said Becky.

"Why mess with a classic?" said Hollins.

I translated Hollins's statement into Xotonian. The Xotonians looked at one another and laughed nervously. Perhaps they expected something more impressive than these four undersized humans.

"I am the king of Earth," said Little Gus, "and I bestow upon you my many magic blessings." I did not translate this.

"Hey! Don't you all have anything better to do?" I yelled at them in Xotonian. The Xotonian gawkers gave a collective shrug and began to slowly disperse.

"It's okay, Chorkle," said Becky, fluffing her hair. "We're the 'kids in space,' remember. We're used to being in the public eye."

"Some of us even enjoy it," said Nicki, rolling her eyes.

"So," I said, "where would you like to go?" So far, we hadn't gotten farther than my dwelling's tiny lichen front lawn.

"Do you guys have Wendy's?" asked Little Gus.

"Not yet," I said.

"How about we go . . . there?" asked Nicky. She was pointing to Dynusk's Column, a massive building that reached all the way up to the ceiling of the giant chamber that contained the city. It was easily the most impressive structure we had, visible from every quarter of Core-of-Rock.

"That's Dynusk's Column," I said. "I don't think humans are allowed inside. The elders would probably call that a security risk. Sorry."

"What's it for?" asked Nicki.

"Surveillance. Inside the Column, the Observers constantly monitor outer space and the rest of Gelo. They use telescopes and radio scanners and stuff. We can keep three eyes on things from way down here because—"

"The Column is wired to sensors that are hidden somewhere on the surface," said Nicki. "That's why it has to go all the way to the roof of the chamber."

"Exactly," I said. She certainly was a quick one.

"Hidden on the surface?" said Hollins. "Everything is always hidden with you guys. Why is that? What are the Xotonians so afraid of?"

"I don't know," I said. "It's just our way of life."

"If you ask me, humankind could use a little more Xotonian subtlety," said Nicki. "Everything we do, we always have to brag about."

"C'mon. We're the best braggers of all time," said Little Gus proudly. "We're totally awesome at it."

"Hiding is just one of many things we do because we believe that Jalasu Jhuk decreed it a long time ago," I said, shrugging.

"Jalasu Jhuk . . . You mean that hologram Xotonian we saw earlier?" asked Becky.

"Yup. To tell you the truth, everybody thought watching space from Dynusk's Column was just another useless tradition too. Until recently."

"When a bunch of two-eyed aliens landed on Gelo?" laughed Hollins.

"Then it didn't seem so useless anymore," I said. "The Observers secretly monitored all your mothership's communications with Eo, you know. Not that they understood what anybody was saying."

"I'm sure most of what you missed was just my mom yelling at the Nolan-Amaral accounting department back home," said Hollins. "They were really tight with the mission budget."

"Well, if Dynusk's Column is off-limits," said Nicki, "maybe there's a biology library or a museum of advanced mathematics we could—"

"I'm starving," said Becky. "How about we try some local cuisine?"

"We could have some more svur-noodles and rild-sauce!" I said, starting back toward the door of my dwelling. "I made extra. We can bring it with us in a moist bag."

"You know, that—that stuff was great," said Becky. "Almost as good as Little Gus Stew. But maybe we should try something different for lunch."

"Hmm. I think I know just the place," I said.

Soon we were standing at Sertor's stall in the middle of the bustling Xotonian marketplace. I ordered five stuffed cave slugs, fully loaded. Sertor was nervous about serving humans at first, but in the end, money was money. Or, more accurately, x'yzoth crystals were money (at least on Gelo).

Again, we had attracted a large crowd of onlookers. They jostled each other for a better view, but they left a bubble of space directly around us. It was as though they thought the humans might turn and bite them at any moment.

"Cer'em," said Hollins, attempting a friendly smile. He'd remembered the Xotonian word for "hello."

The crowd shuddered and began to whisper among themselves. As one might expect, a terrified few began to sob.

We took the slugs to Ryzz Plaza and sat on the stone benches to eat them. Several Xotonians followed us and continued to gape at a distance.

"Good call, Chorkle! These things are delicious," said Becky as she stuffed her mouth with soft, gooey slugmeat.

"They're so . . . tangy." I hadn't told the humans they were eating hollowed-out gastropod mollusks stuffed with fried mold. I'd called them "Xotonian burritos."

"Core-of-Rock is an amazing city," said Nicki, still marveling at Dynusk's Column. "Xotonians have some really impressive technology. So far I've seen super-realistic holograms, handheld blaster weapons, and that weird purple energy field, which I assume somehow cloaks this entire place. It uses tachyonic wave dilution, right?"

"Uh . . . yeah. Of course it does," I said.

"In a lot of ways," said Nicki, "your civilization is much more advanced than ours."

"They don't have Wendy's," grumbled Little Gus quietly. He wasn't enjoying his Xotonian burrito quite as much as Becky was.

"On the other hand, you guys don't have space travel. I mean, besides those three antiques we found back in the . . . secret chamber," said Nicki, lowering her voice for the last two words. "Heck, you guys don't even have cars."

It was true. Xotonians moved around Core-of-Rock by walking. The most rapid transit available was riding on the back of an usk-lizard. And only guards and fungus farmers did that. (Usk-lizards are temperamental, and they stink something awful.)

"It's this weird mix of super advanced and kind of medieval," said Nicki. "Like, how come you have that crazy cloaking shield, but you don't have industrial agriculture? Why are all of your buildings made of simple stone blocks?"

I shrugged.

"Well, who makes all the energy blasters and those little dealies you put in your ear cavity to spy on radio transmissions?"

"Nobody makes them," I said.

"What do you mean?" asked Hollins. "Then where do they come from?"

"I don't know," I said. "We don't really make those things. We just . . . have them."

I could tell that all the humans were deeply confused.

"We can make a stone dwelling or a fence. Well, a stone-mason or a carpenter can. But we only have thirty-one Nyrt-Snoopers. We have two hundred fifty-six energy blasters," I said. "We used to have two hundred fifty-seven, until one of them broke two years ago. It really bummed everyone out."

"So you can't even repair the stuff you already have?" asked Becky.

"Sometimes we can," I said, "if it's a simple problem. A few Xotonians have some understanding of the ancient devices."

"But you can't manufacture anything new," said Nicki.

I shook my head. "These things all come down to us from the Time of Legends. They're special relics that were bestowed upon us by Jalasu Jhuk and its lieutenants. It would take heroes as great as them to make any more. That's what the elders say, anyway."

"Maybe when our parents come back," said Nicki, "we can share some human technology with you. Help you figure out how some of this stuff works."

"Maybe," I said. I'd nearly forgotten the adult humans altogether. If our two species went to war, I doubted that they would want to share anything with Xotonians.

"You know, it's been four days. They should be coming back to Gelo soon," said Hollins. "Do you have any idea what the Council will decide? Will they let us go? If I could just get a message to my mom somehow. Let her know we're safe. It might make things easier. . . ." He trailed off.

"I wouldn't hold out much hope," I said. "My originator is a very tough individual. And Kalac is probably the most compassionate member of the Council—"

"Gah-gah-gah-gah-gah," yelled someone in crude imitation of human speech. "Why don't you talk like a real Xotonian instead of a dirty hoo-min?"

I turned to see, of course, Zenyk. It was standing in the plaza with its usual aspiring bully entourage.

"Hello, Chorkle, old buddy," said Zenyk. "I just came to greet our honored guests."

"Zenyk," I said, "glad to see you. Thank you so much for welcoming them. As always, you are as polite as you are clever."

"Cer'em!" Zenyk yelled, right in Little Gus's face. It startled him and prompted the obligatory joyless laughter from Zenyk's cronies. Hollins and Becky stood up, their fists clenched at their sides. More Xotonians were watching now. Zenyk was making a scene.

"Wow, you seem to be less frightened of humans than your originator was," I said. "You know, Sheln was absolutely terrified." Zenyk scowled.

"Yeah, well, I figured that since you brought them to Core-of-Rock," it said, strutting toward Hollins, "they ought to get the full Xotonian cultural experience. You know?"

Hollins scowled. Though he didn't know what Zenyk was saying, its tone was abundantly clear. The two of them glared at one another. Zenyk was huge for its age, about as big as Hollins.

I put a thol'graz between them, trying to defuse the

situation. An interspecies brawl in Ryzz Plaza would be most unwise. If humans were seen fighting with Xotonians— no matter who started it—things would turn ugly pretty quickly.

"Just say what you mean," I said to Zenyk. "What do you want with us?"

"I think," said Zenyk, poking Hollins right in the chest, "we should all play a friendly game of oog-ball."

CHAPTER TWENTY-SEVEN

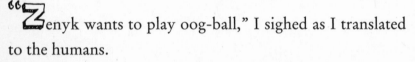

"Zenyk wants to play oog-ball," I sighed as I translated to the humans.

"What's that?" asked Nicki. "I'm usually not so good at anything with the word 'ball' in the name."

Oog-ball is, perhaps, the dumbest sport in the history of the universe. Its object is simple to the point of absurdity. Its method of play is brutal in the extreme. Big Xotonians, like Zenyk, dominate the game. Small, thoughtful ones—like myself, just to pick a random example—have no chance. Among my people, it is insanely popular.

Just how does one play oog-ball? You start with an oog—that's the biggest digestive organ of an usk-lizard. You dry it out, rubberize it, weight it, and inflate it. Now it is a giant ball (an oog-ball, if you will), bigger and considerably heavier than a full-grown Xotonian.

The oog-ball is then placed inside the pel—a tall, circular ring of stalagmites that are spaced so closely together that the ball can't fit between them.

Two opposing teams of five players squeeze through the spaces between the stalagmites and into the pel. Whichever team manages to get the oogball out of the pel is the winner.

That's it. That's the whole game.

If it sounds easy (or, Jalasu Jhuk forbid, fun), trust me, it isn't. The oog-ball barely bounces and, as I said, is incredibly heavy. The teams must work together to climb up the stalagmites and, using their combined strength, hoist the oog-ball over the top.

This would be difficult enough on its own. But it is made considerably more difficult by the inconvenient fact that the other team is pummeling you the whole time. And if you don't want to lose, your team is, of course, pummeling them back.

Oog-ball is a stupid game (that a couple of Xotonians die playing every year). But for whatever reason, it is the great Gelo pastime. My species can't get enough.

I explained all this to the humans as Zenyk and the assembled goons stood by.

"So, yeah," I said, "that's what the game is. And in case I'm not making myself clear: I hate oog-ball."

"I say we play 'em," said Hollins, glowering at Zenyk. "I was captain of the basketball team, the baseball team, and the soccer team at my school. I think I can handle a little 'oog-ball.'"

"I want a piece of these punks," growled Becky.

"Wait, wait," said Nicki. "Aside from getting the ball thingy out of the ring thingy, is there anything else we should know?"

"Each team gets two timeouts," I said.

"C'mon, are you gonna play or what?" cried Zenyk. "I know the big hoo-mins already fled in fear. Maybe these little baby ones are too scared."

"Calm down!" I said. "I'm just explaining the rules."

"Rules?" laughed Zenyk. "Oog-ball doesn't have any rules." I translated this back to the humans.

"Fair enough," said Becky, cracking her knuckles.

"Let's do it," said Hollins.

"I'm down," said Little Gus. "We get kneepads and helmets and stuff, right?"

I didn't say anything.

"I think this is a very, very bad idea," said Nicki quietly.

"Me too," I said.

And so we all walked together to a public pel, just off Ryzz Plaza. The crowd of spectators swelled as we went. A human-Xotonian oog-ball match was bound to attract a lot of interest.

"Chork-a-zoid!" cried one of the many Xotonians following us.

"Linod-tron!" I called back.

"Chorkle, you've got to tell me everything," said Linod as it pushed its way through the crowd toward me. "Sneaking aboard the human spaceship! A daring trek through the Unclaimed Tunnels! Getting interrogated by the Xotonian Council!"

"Sounds like you already know everything."

"Plus, you've got four pet humans now!" said Linod. "Oh please, can I please have one, Chorkle? Please, please, please? I'll even take that little red one." Linod pointed to Gus.

"Sorry, Linod. Afraid I can't spare a single human. You're going to have to find your own."

Linod took me aside and started to whisper. "Fine. Okay. But Chorkle, I came here to warn you. You know how Arani is friends with Chrow's sibling Ukelu, but not like real friends. Like 'sometimes' friends? Anyway, Arani and Ukelu were talking about Chrow, and Chrow said—"

"C'mon, Linod. Get to the point."

"Okay, okay, okay. The word on the street is that this match is just a glorified excuse for Zenyk's team to beat the guano out of all of you. They aren't even going to try to win.

In fact, they want to keep the match going forever, just so they can put the hurt on all of you for as long as possible."

"Hmm. Yeah, that sounds about right," I said.

"So . . . you're obviously going to call the game off, right? Unless you want to die. In which case, can I have your humans?" said Linod. "Except . . . they'll probably all be dead too." Linod sighed.

I explained the situation to the humans. "So the match is a setup," I said. "Zenyk's not even playing to win. I really don't think we should do this."

"Can't back down now," said Hollins, eyeing the crowd. "Too many folks watching. We have to represent humanity. And anyway, it sounds like this creep Zenyk needs to learn a lesson."

"Yeah. There's nothing more satisfying than giving a bully exactly what it deserves," said Becky.

"You don't mess with Earth!" yelled Little Gus, thumping his undersized chest.

"I would really, really prefer not to do this," said Nicki. "If the rest of you suffer a brain injury, no big loss. I mean, except in your case, Hollins. You're obviously really smart too. But I'm a straight-A student! I'm planning to go to Harvard, or at least Dartmouth. Think it through: We don't even know how to play oog-ball. . . ." She trailed off as she realized that her three companions had already made up their minds.

"Oh fine. But when this is done, we are all going to go to the advanced mathematics museum. No arguments," she said. "Can somebody please hold my glasses?"

I gave them to Linod for safekeeping.

Our team tried to meet our opponents on the field of play, but only Little Gus could easily pass between the tightly spaced stalagmites that formed the pel. After much squeezing and tugging—which recalled our journey through the Unclaimed Tunnels and prompted snide jibes from Zenyk and laughter from the crowd—the humans eventually made it inside. It was not an auspicious beginning to the match.

There, in the center of the pel, sat the oog-ball. A big, ugly black spheroid sagging under its own weight. Even rolling an oog-ball was a tough task, much less getting it up over the top of the pel.

Zenyk, Chrow, Skubb, Slal, and Polth were already inside, trying to look tough.

"Good luck," sneered Zenyk to Hollins in Xotonian.

"I'm going to enjoy beating you at your own stupid sport," said Hollins to Zenyk in human.

A rapt sea of Xotonians surrounded the pel now. The atmosphere was electric. Some were merely curious. Most,

I suspected, would love nothing more than to see a bunch of humans get ground into the dirt trying to play our most popular native sport. I heard a few distinctly antihuman chants ("Up with Gelo! Down with Eo!"). Somewhere I heard Linod faintly trying to start a counter-chant of "Oog-ball sucks!" only to be shouted down.

Each member of the other team put a thol'graz on the oog-ball. This was customary. When the last player touched it, the match would begin. Hollins put a hand on. Then Becky. Then Little Gus. Then Nicki.

"Ready?" I said.

They all nodded. I put my thol'graz on the oog-ball—

Suddenly I was in the middle of a chaotic scrum of fly-ing fel'grazes and human elbows and black rubber. I was getting shoved and gouged and kicked away from the center of the ring and toward the pel.

Now my back was crushed against the stalagmites, and my front was crushed by the oog-ball itself. From some-where a thol'graz slapped me. Several stink-glands were discharged—a standard opening gambit in every match I've ever seen. I pushed back as hard as I could against the ball, but it was no use. I wasn't strong enough.

I could barely breathe now. Someone slapped me again. Was that a human hand? Slowly, painfully, I turned my head. I could see Becky beside me. She was also getting crushed between the ball and the pel, but even worse, Chrow had her in a sort of headlock. Two of its thol'grazes were wrapped tightly around her neck.

"Or'on aush!" I called, Xotonian for "timeout."

Whoever was pushing the oog-ball at me stopped. I slumped to the ground and gasped for air.

Our team slowly regrouped on the other side of the pel. After only a few minutes of "play," we looked terrible: already bruised, battered, clothing torn. Hollins even had a bloody nose.

"So this is supposed to be fun . . . how?" asked Little Gus, flexing his shoulder. He seemed to have forgotten his "nobody-messes-with-Earth" persona.

"Did one of you slap me?" I asked.

"I'm sorry. It's really hard to tell all of you apart without my glasses," said Nicki. To her, we Xotonians were now the duplicates.

Becky rubbed her neck. "What's that one called?" she snarled and pointed.

"Chrow," I said.

"Chrow is dead," she said darkly.

"It's okay. It's okay," said Hollins. "This is just the first few minutes of our first time playing this game. We're still learning the ropes. We'll get 'em. Don't you worry." He was leaning his head back and holding a rag to his nose to try to stop the bleeding.

"You're lucky you got hit in the nose," coughed Nicki. "I think somebody sprayed stink on me!"

"Not so funny when you're on the receiving end, is it?" asked Becky. Nicki shook her head and started to retch.

"So do we have a plan?" asked Becky.

"Maybe we can get them to slip on our blood and fall down," said Little Gus.

"Here's what we're going to do," said Hollins. "When the match starts, just let them have the ball. It'll confuse them. At least for a minute."

"That's when we hit them back hard," said Becky, spitting in the dirt.

"Exactly," said Hollins. "Becky, you and I can get in there and scrap with all five of them for a minute. While they're distracted, that's when you three take the ball over the top."

"Wait. Two of you are going to handle all five of them?" asked Nicki.

"Yup," said Hollins. "I was captain of the wrestling team at my school."

"How many teams did your school have?" asked Little Gus.

"A lot of teams. Look, it's simple, guys: Divide and conquer. We can't lose."

When he said it like that, it certainly sounded like a plan!

"Ti'zeg aush," I said. Time in.

Nicki, Becky, and I instantly stepped aside, and Zenyk's team shoved the ball hard. They got no resistance from us and nearly fell forward. The ball rolled against the pel and rolled back at them, throwing them further off balance.

Just as Hollins predicted, this confused them for a split second. Becky took the opportunity to stamp on Chrow's fel'graz and knee it hard in the z'iuk. Chrow slumped to the ground with a gentle groan.

Meanwhile, Hollins flew through the air like some crazed animal. He took a startled Zenyk, Slal, and Polth down with him.

"Okay, this way!" cried Little Gus from somewhere (he was smaller than the oog-ball, so it was easy to lose track of him). Then he, Nicki, and I began to awkwardly roll the oog-ball back toward the pel. Nicki grabbed hold of one of the stalagmites.

"Too slippery!" she said. I had a sinking feeling as I realized that I was the only member of our entire team who was capable of climbing up a three-meter stalagmite. I quickly scaled the pel.

From my vantage point, I could see Hollins. He was on the ground with Polth and Slal in two separate chokeholds and Zenyk in a leglock! Elsewhere, Becky was literally biting Chrow's fribs as it tried to get away from her.

"Hoist it," I yelled. Little Gus and Nicki—probably the two weakest humans—began to lift the oog-ball. Slowly, centimeter by centimeter, the ball rose up the pel; it was above their heads now. I gripped the stalagmites and tried to help from above. Little by little, the oog-ball kept rising! Was there a chance this plan was actually going to work?

The instant this hopeful thought crossed my mind, something heavy knocked me from the pel. It was Skubb.

I lay in the dirt, coughing. Now I could see that Zenyk, Polth, and Slal had apparently broken free from Hollins's holds; the three of them were on top of him in a heap. Becky was chasing Chrow around the pel in a blind rage. Chrow suddenly whirled and threw a thol'graz-ful of dirt in her face. She was temporarily blinded. The oog-ball had fallen, and Little Gus and Nicki were literally trapped under it.

"Or'on aush!" I yelled.

I wouldn't have thought it possible, but our team looked even worse than before. Perhaps because this time morale was much lower.

"So . . . that didn't work," I said.

"My tooth feels loose," whined Little Gus, reaching his hand into his mouth. "Becky, feel my tooth and see if it's actually loose!"

"Yeah. I'm not going to do that," she said, blinking heavily. Tears were running down her face, some combination of the dirt in her eyes and pure, unbridled fury.

Hollins was stanching his nose again. "Look: 'Courage is not having the strength to go on; it is going on when you don't have the strength.' Teddy Roosevelt," he said. "Don't worry, we're gonna win this thing." There wasn't much conviction in his voice.

"Inspiring," sneered Becky. "Any idea how?" Hollins had no answer.

"Guys, I know you're all competitive and stuff, but, seriously, come on," pleaded Nicki. "Somebody threw dirt in Becky's eyes! I got stink-gland sprayed on me! Does this sound like a real sport to anyone else? If we go back out there . . . we're going to get killed."

"We've already used both of our timeouts," I said. "Now there's no way for us to stop them from pounding us forever." Across the pel, the other team stared at us hungrily. No doubt they knew this as well.

"Oog-ball is just a glorified brawl!" said Nicki. "Why would we keep playing a game that has no rules?"

"Wait. That's it," said Hollins. "If there aren't any rules, then . . . then there aren't any rules." A smile slowly spread across his face. The rest of us were deeply confused. Hollins quickly explained his plan.

We resumed our positions. Outside the pel, the crowd roared. I took a deep breath. If this didn't work, we would be stuck in the ring, to be pounded at Zenyk's leisure. Surely the spectators wouldn't let them actually murder us . . . would they?

All of this was racing through my mind as I said, "Ti'zeg aush." The frozen oog-ball tableau sprang to life. Once again we were being pummeled.

Suddenly, Little Gus broke free and ran for his life.

"Please, just leave me alone!" he howled pitifully as he cowered at the opposite side of the pel.

And now the oog-ball was moving again—Slal, Chrow, and Polth were pushing it. Bullies in training, they sensed weakness, and they simply couldn't resist: They were aiming the ball right for Little Gus.

Hollins, Becky, Nicki, and I tried to hold them back, but Zenyk and Skubb were running interference on us at the same time, grabbing at our limbs and faces and anything else they could get their brips on. It was rolling bedlam.

After building up a little speed, the heavy oog-ball

slammed right into Little Gus. The impact knocked him against the pel. Now he was trapped there, squeezed between the stalagmites and the oog-ball itself. The other team kept pushing with all their might, as though they meant to crush him. From somewhere, Little Gus (once more invisible) wailed. There was no way for us to help him.

"Now!" said Hollins, and something shiny flashed in his hand. At this point, instead of pulling at our opponents, we all began to push too. Nine players were now shoving the oog-ball in the same direction, nearly doubling the force. All of it was directed right at poor Little Gus.

Zenyk's team was momentarily too confused to react, but we kept pushing. Over the noise of the crowd, there came a hissing sound, like some colossal sigh. Forward, forward, forward we pushed until we couldn't push any further. Our opponents were fighting back now, but it was too late. We were against the pel.

There, on the other side of the ring of the stalagmites among the crowd, stood Little Gus. We'd squeezed him clear through the gap. In his hands, he held up one corner of the heavy, now deflated oog-ball at his feet. There was a smile on his face.

The crowd exploded.

"We win," I said to Zenyk.

Hollins folded his pocketknife. He'd popped the stupid oog-ball.

"What? That's impossible!" shrieked Zenyk, tears welling in its eyes. "You let all the air out of the—you can't just puncture the—that's against the—"

"Rules?" I said. "Oog-ball doesn't have any rules."

Zenyk was totally speechless. And at that precise moment, I tried to memorize the look on Zenyk's face, to file it away in my fine Xotonian brain for safekeeping. I suspected that this particular memory would keep me warm on cold nights. Brighten my mood in times of despair.

Was popping the oog-ball a low-down, despicable, unfair way to win the match? Absolutely.

And the crowd loved it.

Hollins had come up with a new dirty trick to play out in the pel! That was every serious oog-baller's dream. From now on, deflating the ball would just be another nasty play—like choking and eye gouging and stink-gland discharging—in a sport that was supposed to be nasty. Our victory had, in its own strange way, honored the very spirit of the game.

Now a rhythmic chant began to roll through the crowd: "Human! Human! Human!" (again, the only word of the human language that most Xotonians knew). They hoisted

Little Gus up onto their i'ardas and carried him through the streets. Everyone loves a winner.

Well, not quite everyone. A good third of the spectators were sullen and resentful. They whispered darkly among themselves or whined pitifully. They were angry that a pack of aliens had beaten Xotonians at our own game. But for the moment, they were the minority, and Human Fever carried the day.

We followed the spontaneous parade and rehashed key moments of the match. Linod joined us too, thrilled to have finally played any part—even one as minor as holding on to Nicki's glasses—in an oog-ball victory.

I took one last look back at the pel. Zenyk's team had surrounded it. They were questioning its leadership in what one might call less than deferential tones. In fact, it looked as though things might even turn violent. Now wouldn't that be a shame?

After marching back through Ryzz Plaza and twice around the marketplace, the crowd finally arrived on the lawn of my dwelling for an impromptu celebration.

Little Gus capered and danced. Becky savored the attention (much hair fluffing ensued). Nicki was quiet and mostly stared at the ground, but she had a huge grin plastered on her face the whole time. Hollins even showed off the folding knife and good-naturedly went through all five Xotonian words he could remember about a hundred times. As usual, his accent was terrible, but the Xotonians appreciated the effort. Even Hudka came outside and tried to indirectly take credit for the remarkable human victory.

When the crowd finally dispersed, they shook the humans' hands and said "goodbye." At their request, I had taught them the human farewell.

It was quite a day. If our foray into Core-of-Rock had accomplished anything, it was that maybe, just maybe, a couple hundred Xotonians might despise the human species a little less. At the very least, they had seen that not all of these odd aliens were monsters. And some of them were pretty good oog-ball players.

Shortly after we entered my dwelling, the humans all fell asleep. I couldn't blame them. An oog-ball match would tire out anyone.

Now Hudka and I sat in the living room of our dwelling. Unconscious humans covered most of the furniture.

"You know, they used to call me Hudka the Destroyer, back in my oog-balling days," said my grand-originator. It scratched Pizza's chin as the thyss-cub dozed in its lap. "In one match, I put Gatas right over the pel. Nearly broke its et'vor."

"Why'd you do that?"

"Because Gatas had knocked out three of my ish'kuts by stomping on my face!" said Hudka. "I miss the good old days."

"Speaking of the past," I said, "when we were in the Unclaimed Tunnels, we came to a place I'd never been before. A place I'd never even heard of. It was a forest filled with charred ruins. Hudka, was there another Xotonian settlement once?"

Hudka was quiet for a long time before it spoke. "Yes. Long, long ago."

"But I thought Core-of-Rock was the only Xotonian city."

"Not always. The ruins you saw were once called Flowing-Stone, named for the river that ran through that city. Many thousands lived there. It had its own Stealth Shield. They say it was even greater and more beautiful than Core-of-Rock."

"What happened?"

"In the Time of Legends," said Hudka, "Jalasu Jhuk came from the stars and founded Core-of-Rock to protect the Q-sik. But Jhuk also founded Flowing-Stone for another reason that is now lost to history. The two cities were neighbors, bent toward a common purpose. As you know, Flowing-Stone is only a few hours' walk from here.

"But as the years passed, Core-of-Rock and Flowing-Stone grew apart. That short distance became bigger in the minds of their inhabitants. They became like two different tribes, despite all they had in common. There was a dispute. Some say trade. Others say borders. The true cause is long forgotten. The point is, the two cities went to war."

"Xotonians fought a war among themselves? Why?" I said, astonished. "How could that happen?"

"Imagine two cities, each with a Sheln as Chief of the Council," shrugged Hudka. Put that way, war didn't seem unlikely at all. In fact, it seemed downright inevitable.

"The fighting continued for a few years," Hudka went on, "and Core-of-Rock was losing. So we pressed the one advantage we had. Jalasu Jhuk had put the Vault in Core-of-Rock, not in Flowing-Stone. So we violated our most important commandment. Instead of guarding the Q-sik . . . we fired it."

"And Flowing-Stone was destroyed," I said.

"In an instant," said Hudka, "a beautiful city was burned to ash by the Q-sik's light. It became a place that we don't even tell our young about, because we are too ashamed." I thought back to all the ruined homes I'd seen in the forest, to the Xotonian skull I'd found half-buried in the dirt.

"It was the greatest mistake we ever made. A betrayal of

Jalasu Jhuk," Hudka sighed. "Jhuk always worried about enemies from without. The Great Progenitor never considered the possibility that we could become our own worst enemy. It just shows why the Q-sik is so dangerous."

"Hudka, I saw something else there in Flowing Stone," I said. "A place that wasn't destroyed. I think I know what Flowing-Stone's purpose was. There was a hangar there, and I saw a hologram of Jalasu Jhuk—"

Just then Kalac walked through the front door of our dwelling, and I clapped my gul'orp shut. I was still afraid to mention the starships.

"Well, you look like guano," said Hudka to Kalac, covering my silence. My originator did look thoroughly exhausted. I realized that the Council meeting must have lasted for almost an entire day.

"Thanks," said Kalac, slumping into the single chair that wasn't occupied by a sleeping human. "Why is there a baby thyss-cat in the house?"

"I figured since I already disobeyed you about everything else . . . might as well," I shrugged. Kalac blinked at me. Then it laughed.

Hudka and I looked at each other. Did we just share a synchronized auditory hallucination . . . or had Kalac actually found something funny?

"Do we have any food?" said Kalac. "I feel weak. Twenty-four hours of uninterrupted Sheln can take quite a toll."

"We have most of a stuffed cave slug," I said. Little Gus had only nibbled at his.

"Great," said Kalac. I handed it over, and Kalac devoured it. "Much better," it said.

"So," said Hudka, "what has the just and mighty Council decided to do about the human problem?"

"Will we let them go?" I asked.

"No decision has been reached on that yet," said Kalac. "But I did get them to agree to what I believe is now our best hope for avoiding an outright war. Tomorrow, the young humans may contact their parents."

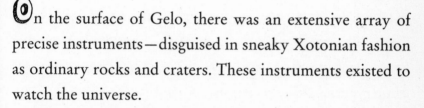

CHAPTER TWENTY-EIGHT

On the surface of Gelo, there was an extensive array of precise instruments—disguised in sneaky Xotonian fashion as ordinary rocks and craters. These instruments existed to watch the universe.

X-rays, radio waves, the ultraviolet, the infrared, and the visible light spectra: All were monitored. The resulting flood of information flowed underground—via ancient wires running through kilometers of solid rock—into a room, a circular chamber in the heart of Dynusk's Column. This room was called the Observatory.

The data gathered above appeared on the countless computer screens that covered every wall of the Observatory. Only now, in addition to tantalizing images of distant galaxies swirling in blackness, the data took the form of numbers and charts and graphs. And it was analyzed by an ancient and erudite order, a priesthood of watchers trained to make sense of it all.

The elders say Jalasu Jhuk's lieutenant, Dynusk, was the first Observer. The hallowed tradition of watching the sky was carried down through the ages to our present time.

What are the Observers looking for, exactly? No one really knows. Yet still they watch.

Now, seven non-Observers—three Xotonian, four human—stood in the Observatory and asked this noble order, for once, not to observe. Instead of using the technology here to gather information, they wished to send it.

"I'm afraid that would be impossible," said Ydar the High Observer, pristine in its clerical robes. "We lack the necessary capacity. Our equipment is very, very sensitive, and I simply cannot allow it."

Several other Observers glared at us from their workstations, computers displaying colorful visual readouts of distant stars.

"I'm sorry if I didn't make myself clear," said Kalac politely, "but this is not a request. They have the Council's permission to contact their mothership. It's important that we let the human leader know that their offspring have not been harmed. That we can reach a peaceful resolution to this situation."

"I deeply wish that it were possible," said Ydar in a tone that suggested quite the opposite, "but alas, at this juncture, it is not." On a nearby desk, Ydar noticed a particularly alluring pie chart of gamma radiation levels in the Ghezs Sector. It quickly hid the chart behind its back.

"Come on," growled Hudka, "I know you're not telling me I walked up five thousand steps to the top of this stupid Column for no reason? These human kids are calling their human parents."

"I would not expect a lay-Xotonian to understand, but our role here is to observe. Not to . . . broadcast," said Ydar, spitting out the last word with disgust.

"Don't you talk to me like I'm some ignorant yokel. My own originator was an Observer, so I know a thing or two about what you lazy mold-brains do up here!" Hudka had gone from annoyed to hopping mad.

"Broadcasting would require alterations to our current observation scheme. It would take away resources that I simply cannot spare," said Ydar. "Remember when the humans landed on the surface? What if we had been broadcasting instead of observing then, eh?"

The other Observers nodded smugly. The day the humans landed on the surface was perhaps the greatest day in the history of the order. It had justified their very existence—

which many Xotonians had come to question—and they weren't about to let anyone forget it.

"We all thank you for your keen observation during the human landing," sighed Kalac.

Ydar continued, "And speaking of humans, I must point out that it is already most unorthodox to bring four of them into the Observatory. What would Jalasu Jhuk have said—"

"Jalasu Jhuk would have said, 'Thank you, Hudka, for smacking that sniveling technocrat until it squealed,'" said Hudka as it started toward Ydar, who stumbled backward in fear. Kalac stopped Hudka and continued to argue with Ydar.

All the while I quietly translated for the humans.

"This Ydar just doesn't want anybody else playing with its precious toys," said Hollins.

"I'm with Hudka," said Becky. "I say we wreck the place." I'd noticed an increased aggression level in Becky since the oog-ball game. Perhaps she had developed a taste for violence?

"Look at that," said Nicki. "A microphone. And that thing's a camera. I'd bet my shrozz'norr mushroom sample on it." Despite the fact that none of us wanted to win that bet, we all looked to where she pointed. In a neglected part of the chamber was a deactivated computer console. Attached to the console was a thin metal cylinder and a small glass orb. "If they have a mic and a camera," continued Nicki, "it means they actually *can* broadcast, not just receive."

"Seriously, I'm trying to avert a war here!" Kalac was almost yelling at Ydar now.

"That is not within the purview of this order. When the war occurs, we will be here to observe it."

"I'm Chief of the Council, you little—"

"Hey, can't the humans call their parents on that?" I said, pointing to the camera-and-mic-equipped computer. Kalac and Ydar stared at me, along with all the rest of the Observers at their workstations.

"Since nobody's using it," I said, shrugging.

"That workstation," cried Ydar, "is out of order!"

I walked over to the console. There was a large green switch on the side. I flicked it. The screen lit up.

"I guess I fixed it," I said.

Ydar sighed. "All right, all right, all right," it said. "But if it gets damaged in any way, then all of you are in grave, unspeakable, historic trouble. And I don't want the humans putting those slimy, wiggly . . . things on my console." I supposed he meant their fingers. Or maybe their tongues?

After a bit of back-and-forth, we eventually agreed that I—presumably less slimy than a human—would physically operate the device. Hopefully, Nicki could tell me how.

"I'm assuming this thing uses high-frequency radio waves," she said. "Those controls over there, they probably move a transmitter somewhere on the surface. Can you ask Ydar?"

After a bit of pleading (and a few more threats from Hudka thrown in for good measure), Ydar agreed to help us. The humans' best guess was that additional vessels had met their mothership to assist with repairs and refueling at some midpoint between Gelo and the human lunar base. So we aimed the transmitter at Earth's moon.

"They planned on landing tomorrow," said Hollins, who watched over our shoulders. "So the ship should be pretty close."

"When I see my dad," said Little Gus, "I'm gonna be all like, 'Hello, Father. When you left, I was but a boy. Now, I am a man.'"

"When I see our parents," said Becky, "I'm going to ask them for a car. Straight up. Emotionally, they're going to be in no position to refuse. I'll be the only eighth grader with a Ferrari."

"Ready?" I said. The humans all nodded. I could see the anticipation on their faces. They missed their parents terribly. "Let's call."

I flicked the switch to begin broadcasting. On the screen

now was a sea of rolling static. Hollins spoke into the microphone: "Hello. This is Daniel Hollins, Nicole García, Rebecca García, and Augustus Zaleski of the Nolan-Amaral mining vessel *Phryxus*. Is anyone out there? Over."

"That knob looks like it might adjust the frequency," said Nicki. "Let's keep trying channels."

Slowly, slowly, I turned the knob, as Hollins repeated his message over and over. Once or twice, the static jumped and almost resolved itself into an image. Each time, I could feel the humans jump with it.

"Where are they?" whispered Little Gus.

Just then, a voice crackled over the device.

"Commander of . . . lan-Amaral mining vessel *Phryxus* . . . who is . . ."

"It's them!" cried Becky.

"Mom?" said Hollins. "Mom, is that you?"

". . . nny . . . is that . . ."

"We need a stronger signal. How do we boost the power?" asked Nicki. I asked Ydar.

"Absolutely not. If that device draws more power, it could short out other—"

"How about I hit your head against that computer until we find the right button?" said Hudka.

"All right, all right, all right! There's a little wheel on the side there. But be careful with it, will you? I don't like the look of your fat, clumsy brips."

Despite the apparent fatness of my brips, I managed to slowly nudge the wheel up.

"Mom," said Hollins, "I just want to let you know that we're all safe. We're with aliens, Mom! But they haven't hurt us. The Xotonians—that's what they call themselves— they're good guys, Mom."

". . . alive! Thank Go . . . aw your SOS . . . safe? . . . back for you . . . your father . . ." the voice crackled.

"Yes, we're safe! Can you hear me? We're safe!"

Slowly, the static resolved itself into a fuzzy image of an adult human female. It was Commander Hollins. Standing over her shoulder was her husband. They both looked incredibly anxious.

The audio was still patchy, though: ". . . not receiving any video . . . Hold on . . . m putting this through to . . . e Garcías . . . and Frank Zal . . . ," said Commander Hollins.

The image on the screen went black for an instant. Then it came back, now divided into four quadrants. The Hollinses were in the upper left square. The other three squares were each occupied by video feeds: another woman and two other men.

"Mom! Dad!" cried Nicki and Becky in perfect unison.

"Hey, Pop!" cried Little Gus. "They have burritos here but they're not very good, and now I have a pet thyss-cat and I named it 'Pizza' and I miss you!"

All the humans—four juveniles and five parents— began to talk all at once. And cry. Even Becky was crying. There was no dirt in her eyes this time.

The quality of the transmission was still terrible, though. It was clear that the *Phryxus* was not receiving any video and only spotty audio. I boosted the power of the signal even further.

"Does the human leader understand that the juveniles haven't been harmed?" asked Kalac. "That there is no need to attack us?" I relayed this to Hollins. He nodded.

"Mom, like I said: We're safe. You don't need the soldiers! We're safe," said Hollins. "Are you hearing me?"

I pushed the power up even further. It was at maximum.

"Hold on, Danny, I think we're getting visuals now."

All five of the adult humans' faces changed from concern to outright terror. "The alien!" cried Commander Hollins. "Danny, it's right next to you!"

The young humans looked confused for a moment. Everyone—including me—had forgotten that I was on camera.

"Oh no, don't worry, Mrs., er, Commander Hollins," cried Nicki. "This is just Chorkle! Chorkle's our friend."

"My second-best friend!" said Little Gus.

Commander Hollins shrieked, "Get away from those children, you—"

And suddenly the signal went dead. The screen was black.

"What happened?" cried Becky.

"Where's my dad?" asked Little Gus.

"Does the human leader understand there is no need for an invasion?" asked Kalac.

"Chorkle, we have to get that signal back!" said Hollins.

I flicked the broadcast button up and down. I played with the signal strength and the frequency. I even moved the transmitter on the surface, tweaking its direction. Nothing changed. The screen was dead.

Everyone waited in quiet anticipation. After a long moment, I heard a soft sound coming from behind me. It was Ydar, sobbing.

"Now that console really is out of order," it said pitifully.

"High Observer Ydar," said one of the other Observers, sitting at its workstation across the chamber.

"What is it, Ghillen? And please don't give me any bad news. We've just lost a console, thanks to these barbarians."

"I've just detected a massive power surge," said Ghillen.

"You see? You see?!" cried Ydar at me, suddenly furious.

"You see what you've done? You and these awful two-eyed monsters. You've used too much power! You've blown out my entire system! By Jalasu Jhuk and all the lieutenants, I curse your—"

"No," said Ghillen. Its screen now showed several little red triangles moving toward a big blue circle.

"I mean that I've detected a power surge in high Gelo orbit. Now I'm seeing . . . ships. Eleven ships. Bearing toward us. Fast."

"It's the humans," said Kalac. "They're here with their soldiers!"

"Negative," said Ghillen.

"What?" I said.

"The ships—the ships don't appear to be human. . . ."

"What are you saying?" said Kalac.

"I don't really know what to make of this, but if our manuals are correct—well, the power surge is consistent with . . ." Ghillen trailed off, its voice filled with terror and uncertainty.

"Spit it out," said Kalac.

"A hyperdrive field," said Ghillen. "Faster-than-light travel."

"Impossible," said Ydar.

"It's not impossible," said Hudka. "It's the Vorem."

CHAPTER TWENTY-NINE

"Do you honestly expect me to believe that we're under attack by a veth-time story invented to scare our offspring into cleaning their chambers?" shrieked Ydar, its voice a mixture of contempt and fear. "Perhaps next you'll tell me that you've found the shugg that lays the x'yzoth crystal egg!"

"See that big triangle on the screen there?" said Hudka, pointing to Ghillen's monitor. "That's the battle cruiser. Just like I saw when I was a kid. And those little ones around it? Those'd be Vorem triremes. A cruiser can generate a hyper-drive field large enough to bring triremes with it. "

"Look, I know you're older than space-dirt, but have you completely lost your mind?" cried Ydar. "Ghillen, check those readings again. I'm sure what we detected was simply a solar flare or some sort of malfunc—"

"High Observer, we're receiving an incoming transmission," said Ghillen.

"What?" squealed Ydar. "Don't answer it."

"They're overriding our—"

Suddenly, the dark screen in front of me came to life once more.

On it was a person—a creature?—covered in sharp, segmented black armor. This armored being sat in a big black chair, aboard a black ship. The dim red lights of computer consoles pulsated in the background.

"Greetings, Xotonian cowards," it said in oddly accented but perfect Xotonian.

"That's not my dad," whispered Little Gus.

"My name is Stentorus Sovyrius Ridian, archon of the Vorem Dominion, general of the Forty-Third Fleet. Humble servant of His Majesty Phaebus Onesius Aetox XXIII, the most glorious imperator of a thousand worlds."

All the thoughts drained from my mind. I was face-to-face with a nightmare come to life. The deep, imperious voice. The chitinous armor. Truly, our legends did not do the Vorem justice.

I stood frozen and unable to speak for several seconds, until Kalac stepped in front of the camera.

"Greetings, General Ridian," said Kalac. "I am Kalac,

Chief of the Xotonian Council. We welcome you to Gelo."

"So this is the fabled Sanctum," said Ridian. "I will admit, I was expecting something more impressive."

"Why have you come here, General?" said Kalac.

"You have something that belongs to us, of course," said Ridian. "We want it back."

"I'm afraid I don't know what you mean," said Kalac. "But we will be happy to make any reasonable accommodations—"

"You know exactly what I mean. We demand the Q-sik."

I felt the bottom fall out of my z'iuk. How could this Vorem know about the Q-sik?

"I know of no such thing," said Kalac.

"I beg to differ. We recently detected an energy spike in this isolated solar system, near this dead, red planet," said Ridian, gesturing toward T'utzuxe. "According to my scientists, the unique properties of this particular spike prove with absolute certainty that it could only have come from one source: the ancient Q-sik. The so-called Universe Ender."

"Again," said Kalac, "if you would tell me what this 'Q-sik' is, then perhaps we could—"

"You're trying my patience, Kalac," said Ridian. "We know the Q-sik is here. You have two options. You can turn it over to us and remain unharmed. Or I can destroy your world with the push of a button. Rest assured, I have the power."

"And why should we give it to you?" cried Hudka, stepping in front of the screen. "The Q-sik is a Xotonian artifact! It's got nothing to do with the Vorem."

"Now we are getting somewhere," said Ridian. "At last I speak to one who acknowledges the truth. Or part of the truth, anyway. The Q-sik is not Xotonian. The idea that your little people could create a device of such power is truly risible."

What was Ridian saying? Of course the Q-sik was Xotonian! How could it not be? It had sat inside the Vault in Core-of-Rock for ages, ever since Jalasu Jhuk had first put it there in the Time of Legends. . . .

"What is all this guano you're talking?" said Hudka.

"Are you telling me that you honestly don't know? Astonishing," laughed Ridian, a thoroughly unpleasant sound. "Well, I suppose that at this point, I lose nothing by explaining. It will help you appreciate the magnitude of my achievement.

"Long ago, a spy for the so-called League of Free Civilizations—a Xotonian starship captain called Jalasu Jhuk—managed to steal the Q-sik from the Vorem Domin-ion. We conquered Jhuk's homeworld, but it nevertheless managed to elude us and hide the device somewhere in the vastness of the universe. Your asteroid is that somewhere."

All the Xotonians in the room were dumbstruck. Could Ridian really be telling the truth? Was our Great Progenitor actually an agent for something called the League of Free Civilizations? Jhuk's holographic recording had mentioned a league, but . . . what was it?

"Bah," cried Hudka. "Now I know you're lying. You never conquered Gelo."

"Have you been hiding in your little hole for so long that you've actually forgotten who you are? Why you're here? Surely you realize that this asteroid, this space rock, is not your true home."

Hudka said nothing. Our legends had it that Jalasu Jhuk traveled the stars. We'd never stopped to consider that Jhuk might have come from somewhere else first.

"Brilliant," mused Ridian. "The Sanctum must have been deliberately isolated from the rest of the universe, the better to conceal its existence. I'd wager you don't even have space travel, do you?"

Again, Hudka said nothing.

"You don't," said Ridian. "You've been completely cut off. Hiding in the darkness here through the long years, while history marched onward. All the more impressive then that I, alone, have found you at last. And as an added bonus, this solar system contains another fully populated world, as yet unconquered by the Dominion. It will be ours as well." He meant Eo.

"So why do you need the Q-sik?" I blurted out, surprising even myself.

Ridian stared at me for a moment. "Why does this child address me?"

"Kid makes a fair point," said Hudka. "If the Dominion is so tough—conquered all these planets, blah, blah, blah—then what's one more weapon to you? Who cares?"

"Because there are still a few deluded insurgents out there, hiding on scattered worlds, who refuse to accept Dominion rule. Rest assured, the imperator could crush them at his leisure. History shows that we have done so countless times before. But our sovereign is most compassionate. He wishes to conquer them without a regrettable loss of life. When we have the fabled Q-sik, all will give up hope of resisting us."

"And you guys spent thousands of years looking for this thing?" I said. "Why don't you just make another one?"

"I have no reason to answer more of your questions," said Ridian. "In fact, they are beginning to annoy me."

"You can't. Can you?" I said.

"How dare you question the power of the—"

"You're just like us," I said. "You don't understand how the Q-sik works either. If you did, you could just create a new one. But you don't, so you can't. The Q-sik might not be ours, but it's not yours either. I know that now."

"Regardless," said Ridian, "we will take it from you. Again, I repeat my offer: Give us the Q-sik, and we will leave you there to enjoy your little lives in peace. If you don't, I will use my ship's arsenal of nuclear weapons to knock your little asteroid out of orbit. It will burn to nothing as it falls to the surface of the red planet. You have one day to decide. We await your response."

"I have an answer to your question, Ridian," said Hudka. "We know why we're here: to keep the Q-sik from the likes of you!"

"Really? If you had not used the device, we would be searching still," laughed Ridian. And the screen went dark.

CHAPTER THIRTY

A silence hung over the Observatory. The screens on the walls now showed visible-light-spectrum feeds of the Vorem flotilla. Ridian's battle cruiser was a jagged hulk bristling with weapons, somehow blacker than the space around it. Nearby flitted the smaller, more agile triremes. They practiced sharp military formations and precise astronautic maneuvers. I supposed these demonstrations were meant to terrify us further. Speaking for myself, I was already plenty terrified.

At last, Little Gus spoke. "So what the heck was that all about? That dude looked, like, super evil."

I roughly translated the exchange for the humans.

"So these Vorem plan to attack Earth as well," said Hollins grimly.

I nodded.

"And by the looks of it," said Nicki, "their weapons are

far beyond anything we have back home. I wonder if Earth could hold them off for five minutes. I mean, they have faster-than-light travel. That's crazy. . . ." She trailed off as she noticed everyone staring at her. "You know . . . thinking out loud," she shrugged.

"What did he mean when he said you had 'used the device'?" asked Becky.

I sighed. I didn't want to tell them, but they needed to know. "We—we fired the Q-sik to destroy the tunnels underneath your mothership. That's what caused the asteroid-quake."

"You mean . . . you used it on us?" she said. "We could have all died, you know. We almost did." I could see pain growing in her eyes. "Why didn't you at least try talking to us first?"

"Some of us wanted to," I gestured to Hudka. "But we held a vote, and the majority of Xotonians decided on a—a different plan."

"Well, then the majority of Xotonians are no better than that creep in the armor!" she snapped.

"You might be right," I said.

"Chorkle, I know this may not be the best time," said Hollins, "but we need to get back into contact with my mom, with the *Phryxus*. We have to warn them that these Vorem guys are here now."

I asked Ghillen.

"Negative," said Ghillen, shaking its head. "The Vorem are somehow jamming all external communications. It looks like the only outgoing call we can make is to Ridian's battle cruiser."

"Sorry," I said to Hollins. He nodded. I could tell he was disappointed, but he put on a brave face.

I looked at Kalac. My originator still stared at the empty screen where the dark general had appeared moments before; its expression was grim.

"We should have listened to you," said Kalac. "We used the Q-sik, and it brought our enemies here. We should have listened to you. To both of you."

I expected Hudka to pile on, to give Kalac the traditional I-told-you-so treatment, only times a hundred. But Hudka said nothing.

Kalac addressed everyone in the room. "I'm going to call another Grand Conclave. Ydar, can we get the live feeds from your telescopes down to Ryzz Plaza? Otherwise no one will believe that the Vorem are actually real. Honestly, I can barely believe it myself."

"It can be done, Chief," said Ydar. There was no whining or resistance in the High Observer's voice now.

"Good. Bring whatever else is necessary for outgoing communication as well."

Ydar nodded.

"Everyone, please gather in one hour," said Kalac. "And spread the word." Then it turned and abruptly left the Observatory.

Hudka, the humans, and I followed behind, down the endless spiral staircase that lead to the bottom of Dynusk's Column. We soon lost sight of Kalac, though. My originator was practically running.

"You should give the Vorem general the stupid Q-sik," said Becky as we walked. "I don't want to die over some fight that you guys probably started in the first place."

Had we started the fight with the Vorem? It turned out there was a lot we didn't know about our own past.

No one else spoke during our long descent except Hudka, who occasionally complained about its aching fel'grazes. I believe this grumbling was for my benefit. My grand-originator was trying to enforce some sense of normalcy on a universe that suddenly seemed insane. But I could tell that old Hudka's is'pog wasn't in it.

By the time we reached Ryzz Plaza, it was nearly full. I guess news travels fast—when that news is that monsters are real and that they've come to destroy you.

Kalac stood quietly beneath the statue of Jalasu Jhuk, watching the crowd swell. One by one, my originator was joined by Glyac, Dyves, Loghoz, and, at last, Sheln.

Loghoz looked around. "By Great Jalasu Jhuk of the Stars," it cried, "let this, the eight hundred eighteenth Grand Conclave of the Xotonian people, commence! The first to speak will be Kalac, the Chief of the Council!" I quietly translated the proceedings for the humans.

"By now you've probably heard the rumors," said Kalac. "I am here to confirm that they are true. The Vorem are real. They are here. And they want the Q-sik."

Total silence descended on the plaza. There was no whispering or murmuring now. Six thousand Xotonians stared back at Kalac, utterly lost. They wanted someone to protect them. To save them from a waking nightmare.

"All right. As usual, I guess it's up to me to inject a little common sense into the proceedings," said Sheln. "We know what those Observers say they think they may have seen. But I guess I need to remind everyone that we still face a clear and present danger. An immediate threat that we know is real. Folks, it's called the hoo-mins. They're coming back!"

Becky scowled as I translated this part.

"In fact, I, for one," continued Sheln, "have to object to the fact that there are four hoo-mins here, right now, spying on this Grand Con—"

"Quiet, Sheln!" screamed someone from the crowd.

"Shut your fat gul'orp, you moron!" cried someone else.

"The Idiot Conclave is one block over!" yelled a third.

Surprisingly, none of these outbursts came from Hudka.

"I understand your skepticism," said Kalac. "High Observer Ydar, please show them."

Ydar, standing nearby, nodded and wheeled forward a large rolling view-screen (the very same one that Kalac had used to make the asteroid-quake presentation). Ydar punched a button, and the display switched to a live feed from the surface telescopes. The menacing bulk of the Vorem battle crusier now filled the screen.

Somewhere, a Xotonian child shrieked. In an instant, there was complete pandemonium in the plaza. Many began to convulse with uncontrollable fear. Others fainted where they stood. Several fights broke out. A few Xotonians simply ran off. The sight of their deepest fears made real was too much to bear.

"Please try to remain calm," yelled Kalac over the sound of the crowd's anguish. "I want all of you to know that I accept full responsibility for this situation. The Vorem leader, General Ridian, revealed that they were able to locate the Q-sik when we fired it a few days ago. As you know, this was part of the plan—my plan—to rid Gelo of the human miners. You placed your trust in me as a leader, and I failed you. For that, I am truly sorry."

At this, many paused uneasily. Despite what Kalac had said, they must have known that they bore a share of the responsibility as well. After all, they had voted for it.

"Ridian has given us an ultimatum," Kalac continued. "He says that if we give him the Q-sik, we will be spared. If not, he will destroy Gelo. I don't have a reason to doubt that he has the power. We need to make a decision."

"Well, I, for one, find this to be an incredibly easy choice," shrieked Dyves, its four thol'grazes flapping wildly. "We should give Ridian what he wants, and then go on with our lives. I fail to see how this solution isn't completely obvious."

"Agreed!" moaned Loghoz. "Looking at that battle cruiser, I see an enemy that is far, far more advanced than the humans of Eo. Realistically, how can we hope to resist a species that can travel faster than the speed of light?"

"If the Vorem are real," said Dyves, "then who knows what else from the old stories is true? Maybe they can raise the dead and breathe fire too!"

The crowd seemed to be persuaded. Raw hysteria had given way to hushed terror. Fear always has its appeal for crowds of Xotonians.

"Are you two kidding me?" someone cried out. "The more you talk, the more I think Sheln might not actually be the dumbest member of the Council." This time, of course, it was Hudka.

Loghoz sighed. "Surprise, surprise: Hudka wants to talk," it said. "If the Council agrees, Hudka may address the Grand—"

Hudka didn't wait for a vote. "We cannot give up the Q-sik to the Vorem! That Ridian is meaner than a thyss-cat, but he knows a thing or two that we don't. Sure, it's always been our musty old tradition to guard the Vault. But did we ever think about why? I now believe it's the whole reason we're here. Gelo was Jalasu Jhuk's hiding place for the Q-sik. It's why we exist!"

"What do you mean 'why we exist'?" said Dyves. "We don't exist for a particular reason any more than—than nosts do." Dyves pointed to a clump of the small white mushrooms growing nearby.

"No," said Hudka. "I mean that it's why we exist on Gelo. All those legends about the evil Vorem chasing Jalasu Jhuk all over space before it came here, why, I think they're true too! Jalasu Jhuk stole the Q-sik and then found the perfect hiding spot for it: an insignificant asteroid in the middle of nowhere. Astronomically speaking, that is. Then wily ol' Jhuk left some Xotonians here to guard it: our ancestors."

"Pardon me," said Glyac, who had remained calm (or perhaps asleep) so far. "But wouldn't that imply that there could be other Xotonians out there in the universe?"

Hudka shrugged. "I don't know about that. I suppose it's possible. But I do know that our Great Progenitor's top priority was keeping the Q-sik from the Vorem. I'm starting to suspect that it's more powerful than we ever imagined."

"Speaking as one who has fired the Q-sik," said Kalac, "I can attest to that. We used the minimum power setting on the device, yet it still vaporized kilometers of solid rock in an instant. And where we fired, it created a—a rip in space. A tiny wormhole, no bigger than the tip of my brip. This wormhole sealed itself almost immediately in a burst of dark energy, but the effect was . . . . incredible. Terrifying."

"Exactly why we can't let them have it!" said Hudka. "If we give it over to them, then who knows how much destruction they will cause?"

"Pardon me, but who cares?" cried Loghoz. "If we don't give up the Q-sik, it doesn't matter. We'll all be dead! If I understand your argument, you're asking us to concern ourselves with some hypothetical future danger instead of our own immediate and certain destruction! How does that make any sense at all?"

At this, the crowd began to mumble. There was a certain logic to Loghoz's position.

"Look, everybody knows I'm no fan of the Vorem," said Sheln, "but these are extraordinary times. I say we contact this Ridian and propose an alliance against the hoo-mins. We can fight those two-eyed freaks together!"

The crowd erupted in disdain at Sheln's obvious over-reach.

"Uh, excuse me," said Hollins quietly. I translated his words into Xotonian.

"Can I have, er, permission to address the, uh, Conclave?" asked Hollins, speaking more loudly now. The Xotonian populace grew quiet.

"Absolutely not!" cried Sheln. "Now the hoo-mins want to dictate our domestic policy? Out of the question!"

"We should listen to the boy," said Hudka.

"He's a real oog-baller! Let him talk!" cried someone from the crowd.

"If the Council agrees," said Kalac, "the human Hollins may address the Conclave. All in favor?"

A quick vote was held. The result was three to two in favor, with Sheln and Loghoz voting against.

Hollins cleared his throat. "Cer'em," he said. He was still pronouncing it wrong, but the crowd gave a light acknowledgment of his effort. Hollins certainly had gotten a lot of use out of that one word.

"With all due respect," he continued, "Ridian isn't going to destroy Gelo. Not yet, anyway."

"Oh, so hoo-mins can read minds now?" said Sheln.

"They can?" said Dvyes, clapping its thol'grazes over its head for telepathic protection.

"Hey, hoo-min," said Sheln, "I'm thinking of a color right now. What color could it be?"

"Stupid isn't a color! Cram it, you shaved cave-ape!" This time it was me yelling at Sheln, in a clear departure from my role as translator.

Hollins was surprised by my outburst, but he continued. "Look, Ridian won't destroy Gelo before he gets what he wants. Because doing that would mean destroying the Q-sik itself."

"So? Who knows what these Vorem are capable of?" asked Dyves.

"What we do know is that they've apparently been looking for this thing for a long, long time. That means they want it really badly. Ridian won't risk losing it. On the other hand, once you give it up, then Ridian has no reason not to destroy Gelo. The Q-sik is the only leverage you have over him. Turning it over is a bad move, strategically."

"He's right," said Kalac.

"That means they'll need to come down here and get it," said Hollins. "If they invade, you can at least fight back."

"How?" cried Loghoz, bursting into tears. "At least we have better weapons than the humans, but how can we possibly fight . . . that?" It pointed to the battle cruiser in despair. The jagged black ship, thick with guns, looked like death incarnate.

"Permission to address the Council?" I said. "Not as a translator, I mean."

"Oh, great," said Sheln. "Let's all hear what the littlest hoo-min lover has to say."

"I think there is a way for us to fight," I said. What I was about to say next was a risk, but I had no choice. "In the Unclaimed Tunnels, there are ruins—a place we once called Flowing-Stone—and there we found ships—three armed starfighters. I think we can get them up and running."

Once more the crowd lost control. The idea of actual star-fighters existing on Gelo was incredible. It changed every-thing. Those who had fainted before fainted again. And a few new fights even erupted.

"Ridian doesn't know that we have them," I yelled over the uproar. "We can surprise him."

"Our tunnels are defensible," said Hudka. "We know

them like the back of our thol'grazes, but the Vorem will be stumbling around in the dark. With the starfighters—"

"Look, if these starfighters actually exist—which I severely doubt," said Sheln, "then we should use them to attack the humans!" More booing from the crowd.

"Aha! So you do know how to say the word correctly!" I yelled.

"I meant 'hoo-mins'! Whatever! Shut up!"

"But speaking of the humans," said Dyves, its eyes moist, "doesn't Kalac's previous point about fighting a war hold true here too? Even if, by some miracle, we were able to fight off this awful Vorem attack, now they know where to find us. What's to stop them from coming back until they win? What's the use?"

"I'm not so sure that the rest of the Vorem do know where we are," said Kalac. "Ridian seemed awfully proud of having found Gelo all by himself. Something tells me he hasn't shared the location with others of his kind, lest someone else steal the credit."

"Hmm," said Hudka. "If the old stories are true, then the little ships—the triremes—don't have faster-than-light capability. Only the battle cruiser can generate a hyperdrive field. So if we could just take out the battle cruiser quickly enough—its hyperdrive and communications systems, at least—then word would never get back to the ol' Vorem imperator on the other side of the galaxy. The location of Gelo would remain a secret!"

More noise from the crowd, approving now. They were warming to the idea.

"The point is, we have a chance," I said. And with that, I explained to the gathered crowd the rest of my plan.

When I was done, Kalac addressed the Conclave. "The time has come for us as a people to make a decision," said Kalac. "Do we give up the Q-sik and hope to be spared, or do we fight the Vorem knowing full well . . . that we may not prevail?"

And so the Xotonian people chose, by a vote of 5,872 to 217, to fight.

CHAPTER THIRTY-ONE

"What happened?" asked Nicki as the Conclave began to disperse.

"We're going to war," I said.

The crowd in the plaza was thinning. All able-bodied adult Xotonians were to report back in one hour to begin training and preparation for the defense of our tunnels. There was much work to do.

"Though it's impossible to know, I believe we've made the right decision," said Kalac, walking toward us. "Chorkle, I want to thank you and Hollins for speaking up."

"You're welcome," I said.

"You know, I think one day you'll be a better Chief of the Council than I am," said Kalac. I was shocked. Kalac thought I was capable of leading the Xotonian people?

"But right now, we have our work cut out for us," said

Kalac. "I can't believe we actually have starships—a secret you should not have kept from me, by the way. But I'm not so sure how we'll use them. It's been many ages since the time of Jalasu Jhuk. None of us knows how to fly the things."

"No," I said, "but they do." I pointed to the young humans.

"Are you sure that they want to help us?" asked Kalac. "They'd be risking their lives, and, honestly, we haven't done much to earn their goodwill."

I sighed. Kalac spoke the truth.

"I can ask," I said. And I did.

"Chorkle, speaking for myself, I just want to go home," said Nicki. "Our parents are going to be here so soon."

"Not soon enough," said Hollins. "If Ridian keeps his word, the Vorem invasion of Gelo will already be underway by the time they return. The Vorem will attack here, and then they'll move on to Earth."

"But . . . we're just kids," said Nicki.

"Yeah," said Hollins. "And right now we're also the best chance the human race—and the Xotonian race—have got. 'Do what you can, with what you have, where you are.' That was T.R.'s motto." He turned to me. "You can count me in, Chorkle. The Vorem need to be stopped."

"I'm in too," said Nicki. "I'm ninety percent sure I can

bring those ships back online but . . . I'm no great pilot. I don't think I can fly a starfighter."

"Each ship will need a gunner too," I said. "And nobody is better than you at shooting down alien spaceships."

"Chorkle, Xenostryfe III is a video game!" she said.

"Exactly," I said. "Reality won't stand a chance."

Nicki sighed and then nodded.

"Well, I, for one, am an excellent pilot," said Little Gus, attempting to balance Hudka's cane on his outstretched finger as Hudka struggled in vain to get it back. "I'd be happy to fly a super dangerous and technically difficult combat mission."

Immediately, I thought back to Little Gus wedging his rocket-bike between the two boulders of Jehe Canyon, his 22 percent pilot test score, his uncanny ability to shoot his own teammates in Xenostryfe III.

I said, "Well, maybe you, er—"

"Gus . . . I can't let you go into a war," Hollins said, placing a hand on Little Gus's shoulder.

"What?" cried Little Gus, shrugging off Hollins's hand. "What are you talking about, dude?"

"I'm sorry," said Hollins. "But you're only ten years old. If you got hurt, your dad and my mom would fight each other to see who gets to kill me first."

"But you're just thirteen! Nicki's twelve! Are you telling me twelve is somehow the magic space war cutoff age? I want to help!"

"If we're being honest, there's a big chance that this plan won't work. If the worst happens," said Hollins, "we can't all be aboard those starfighters. At least one of us needs to survive this for the sake of all our parents and the people watching back on Earth. You have to stay back here, where it's safer. I'm sorry." Little Gus growled and swung Hudka's cane hard, knocking a stone across the plaza. He looked more dejected than I'd ever seen him.

Last was Becky.

"So you want me to fight the Vorem, risk my life to help the Xotonians so that they can turn around and attack the human race again, like Sheln wants," said Becky. "Yeah, no thanks. This isn't our war."

"I know you're still angry about the asteroid-quake," I said. "I would be too. We made a bad decision because we were afraid."

"Chorkle, you've been kind to me. Helped us all a lot. I consider you a friend," said Becky. "But as for the rest of your species, I look at them and I see a clannish, small-minded group that lashes out at anyone different from themselves."

"But don't you get it?" said Nicki. "We acted the same way toward Chorkle at first. You saw how our parents freaked out when—"

"No, she's right," I said. "At our worst, we do act this way. But I believe we're capable of doing better. And I'm not the only one. Think of Hudka or Linod or the crowd that carried Little Gus through the streets. All I can tell you is that we're not all bad. Nobody is. Not humans. Not Xotonians."

"Look, Becky," said Hollins, "like it or not, the Vorem will be here before our parents. If they succeed in conquering Gelo, then it won't matter anyway. We'll be prisoners . . . or worse. I trust the Xotonians a lot more than I trust the Vorem. And as long as we're on this asteroid, our fate is tied to these aliens."

"Well, maybe the Xotonians should have thought of that before they tried to kill us."

"Trust me, sis. I don't want to fight either. But they're going to attack Earth next. And unless we can stop them here, they'll have the Q-sik when they do."

"Well, maybe the Vorem, at least, will have the courage to attack us with it directly."

I translated her response back into Xotonian for Kalac. Kalac nodded slowly.

"I understand. And if I were her, I don't know if I'd consider the Xotonians worth helping," said my originator. "But would you please tell her that, whatever she decides to do . . . I'm sorry."

I did.

Becky paused for a long moment. "Thank you," she said at last.

"Look," said Hollins, "I'm about to say something that I am probably going to regret. Something that I probably won't hear the end of for the rest of my life. Words that are going to cause me physical pain to utter."

He gulped. We all waited.

"Well?" said Becky.

"Becky," he said, "there's a small chance that . . . by a certain definition . . . you might be . . ." He trailed off.

"Excuse me?"

"C'mon. Please don't make me repeat it."

Becky waited again.

"Ugh. Okay. You are a better pilot than me. There! Are you happy? You're a better pilot than me. And I don't think we can do this without you."

"You know," said Becky, grinning, "I'd already made my mind up to help after Kalac apologized. But thanks for telling me. Good to know."

"Yes!" I screamed and turned a triple backflip. With Becky and Hollins, we could at least get two of the starfighters in the air.

"Great. Everyone gets to go but me," said Little Gus, and he threw Hudka's cane hard at the ground.

"Yo, sorry," he said as he sullenly picked it up and handed it back to my grand-originator.

We were mostly alone in the plaza now. Along with a few stragglers, only Ydar and the large view-screen remained. On it, the battle cruiser still floated ominously, red lights blinking.

"Okay," said Kalac. "Shall I inform Ridian of our decision?"

"What?" cried Hudka. "Why in the name of Morool would you tell that monster anything?"

"I've learned my lesson," said Kalac. "I'm not going to start a war without trying to talk first. I need to give Ridian the chance to back down. The stakes are too high."

"You know . . . you're right," said Hudka. For the record, it was the only time in my memory when I'd heard Hudka say this phrase to Kalac.

"High Observer Ydar," said Kalac, "is it possible to contact Ridian from here?"

"Sure, Chief," said Ydar. "Just give me a moment." Ydar plugged in the camera and microphone, fiddled with a few settings on the screen, and pounded the side of the screen once for good measure.

"Okay," said Ydar. "Calling now."

There was a moment of static. Then the screen showed the armored general. He was scarcely less frightening than his jagged black ship.

"Hello, General Ridian," said Kalac.

"Greetings, Kalac, Chief of the Council," said Ridian. "I take it you have decided to give up the Q-sik."

"We have decided to do no such thing. I'm contacting you to give you the chance to abandon your current course of action. We don't have to fight. I believe we can have peace."

"Indeed, it will be most peaceful when all of you are dead. Shall I arm my nuclear missiles and destroy you?" His hands danced across the instrument panel in front of him.

"Perhaps you can do that, but I don't think that you will. I think you want the Q-sik too badly to destroy it. So I guess you'll have to come down here and get it."

Ridian paused. "You've called my bluff. You are correct. In approximately twenty hours, I will, indeed, land troops on your asteroid, enter your tunnels, and bring the Q-sik back out."

"I must warn you that will be no easy feat," said Kalac.

"Good. To be perfectly honest, I hoped you wouldn't give it up without a fight," laughed Ridian. "There is more glory in an invasion. My son will be leading it, you know. It will give him his first taste of battle, of true command. An opportunity to prove whether he is weak or strong."

"All the more reason to call this whole thing off," said Kalac. "No reason for you to risk your son's life. Or to endanger the life of my own offspring. All of our offspring."

"I disagree. We have a saying on Voryx Prime: My triumph is your blood."

"I wish you'd reconsider, Ridian. I believe the universe is big enough for Vorem and Xotonian and human too."

"Wrong," said Ridian. "There is only one universe. It belongs to us." And the screen went dark.

"Nice guy," said Hudka. "We should consider inviting him over for the next Feast of Zhavend."

"We don't have much time now," said Kalac. "We need to get our defenses in order and try to bring those starfighters online."

"Eromu!" Kalac called out, seeing the guard on its usk-lizard across the plaza.

Eromu trotted closer. "Yes, Chief of Council?" It eyed the young humans, especially Hollins—who had once held it at blaster-point—with suspicion.

"Bring more usk-lizards from the guardhouse stables. We need to get to the ruins of Flowing-Stone, fast."

"Very well, Chief," said Eromu, and it galloped off.

"Tell the human children to ready themselves," said Kalac to me.

"Before we go," I said to Kalac, "there's one more thing we need." And I pointed to the Vault.

CHAPTER THIRTY-TWO

Becky eased up the vertical thrusters. Slowly, slowly, the Xotonian starfighter began to float upward.

"It's working!" I cried. We were hovering about five meters off the floor of the hangar now.

"And forward thrusters," came Nicki's voice over the com. Becky nudged the throttle, and the ship began to slowly float forward.

"Now stop," said Nicki, and we did.

"And roll."

Becky gently wiggled the control stick right then left. The whole ship rolled from side to side.

"Pitch," said Nicki.

Becky pushed the stick forward, bringing the nose of the ship down. She pulled it backward, bringing the nose up.

"And yaw," said Nicki.

Becky twisted the stick, and the nose of the ship turned right and left.

"Looking good," said Becky. "I'm bringing her down now." Ever so gently, Becky set the ship back onto the floor of the hangar. She really was a good pilot.

It had taken many hours, but the third starfighter was finally online.

For the first time in centuries, the iridium hangar beneath the ruins was alive with activity. It had become part workshop, part command center.

Nicki had been coding furiously—sometimes on both holodrives at once—ever since we'd arrived. Four Observers, including Ghillen, had accompanied us. Of all Xotonians, their understanding of our ancient technology was the greatest. They offered advice and assisted Nicki where they could, especially in creating a communication link between the ships and the Observatory.

A tiny screen in the cockpit crackled on, and Ydar's face appeared on it. "Hello, this is High Observer Ydar. Do you read me?"

"Hey, Ydar!" I said. Ydar frowned. "I mean, greetings, High Observer," I said. "We read you loud and clear."

"All this . . . broadcasting," chuckled Ydar. "I'm worried

I'm going to develop a taste for it. Anyway, your ships will have our eyes and ears here in Core-of-Rock and on the surface as well, if you need them."

"Is it possible to contact the human ship, *Phryxus*?"

"I've tried. But so far, no luck. Ridian is still jamming all our external communications," said Ydar. "I'll keep at it, though. If I can get a hold of the humans, I'll patch them through directly. Ydar out."

The time of the invasion was approaching fast. Again and again we discussed and refined the plan. We would wait until Ridian had landed the troops on Gelo with his triremes. Then, once the Vorem were fully engaged in our tunnels, we would launch a surprise attack against the un-protected battle cruiser. We hoped that if we hit it hard and fast, we could take out the ship's hyperdrive and communi-cations systems.

Hollins would fly the first fighter, and Nicki would be his gunner. She didn't seem excited to put her Xenostryfe III skills to the ultimate test, but this was mitigated by a strange eagerness to spend time alone with Hollins. Very odd.

Becky would fly the second fighter with Kalac on board. My originator would not be the gunner, however. That role would be filled by—you guessed it—me. Kalac protested at first, until I performed a quick demo of my Xenostryfe capabilities on Nicki's holodrive. Kalac conceded that I was qualified. I got a score of 1,672,890, a personal best.

Despite a total lack of experience, two brave Xoto-nians—Ornim and Chayl—had volunteered to fly the final starfighter.

Ever the optimist, Hollins hoped to give them a crash course in piloting. But in the end, they simply couldn't get the hang of it. While Hollins was trying to explain some basic astronautic concept, Chayl lost control of the ship and rammed it into one of the walls of the hangar, nearly killing us all. The ship suffered only minor damage, and no one was hurt, but it was the end of their flight training.

"Maybe if I had two months," sighed Hollins. "But either of them in the cockpit . . . is going to be more of a liability than a help."

"If only Nicki had some sort of flight simulator game on her holodrive, then maybe I would know how to fly a spaceship right now," I said. "Instead I only know how to race cars in endless circles in 'Indianapolis.'"

"Maybe that'll come in handy one day," said Hollins, shrugging. He sounded doubtful.

So Ornim and Chayl reluctantly returned to Core-of-Rock on the back of an usk-lizard. There, they could at least contribute to the general defense.

I worried about the Xotonian city. Even if we succeeded in disabling or destroying the battle cruiser, Core-of-Rock could still be overrun with Vorem legionaries. I hoped Hudka and Little Gus would remain safe.

Little Gus had protested mightily when Hollins had insisted he stay behind.

"Come on, man! I want to help. Just let me help," Little Gus had said, standing in the doorway of my dwelling. "I'm old enough. I'll be eleven soon!"

"I'm sorry Gus," Hollins had said quietly.

And Little Gus had stared at the ground, tears shining on his cheeks. Hudka tried to comfort him, but when Nicki told them we'd need to take both holodrives with us, they both began to wail in despair. For Hudka and Little Gus, there would be no video games for the duration of the battle. War is hell, as the human expression goes.

Indeed, Nicki was now using both holodrives. The ships were operational. Communications were online. But there was one thing left to do.

Ghillen and the other three Observers were working with her to modify Becky's starfighter. On the nose of the ship, with the help of welding torches and wires and Jalasu Jhuk's ancient manual, they had mounted the Q-sik.

CHAPTER THIRTY-THREE

The hatches of the triremes fell open, and dozens of Vorem legionaries poured out. They wore heavy segmented black armor and carried blaster rifles. They were a fighting force that had conquered countless worlds before. Across the blue-gray surface of Gelo they marched, bearing the battle standard of General Stentorus Sovyrius Ridian. It was as grim as you might have expected: three black suns on a field of red.

In tense silence, we watched the invasion on a view-screen. The feed had been piped to the hangar from the surface, via the Observatory.

Ridian had only landed five of his ten triremes for the invasion. The other five remained in orbit near his ship.

"Well," sighed Hollins, "I guess the battle cruiser won't be unprotected after all."

"I hope the mighty Daniel Hollins isn't afraid," said

Becky. I couldn't speak for anyone else, but the mighty Chorkle was terrified. To calm my mind, I tried to focus on the memory of Zenyk's face as we won the oog-ball match.

On the screen, a centurion used a handheld scanning device to locate one of our surface hatches. He quickly reported his findings back to a slender Vorem in ornate armor and a heavy crimson cloak, the legate leading the invasion. Was this Ridian's son?

The legate nodded, and the centurion flung the hatch open. Down the Vorem legion marched, into the darkness.

"The Stealth Shield ought to conceal the general underground location of Gelo, but . . . it won't be long now," said Kalac.

Periodically, the Observers changed the view-screens to different feeds. At several points on the surface, the same scene was repeating itself. The Vorem were invading the Gelo cavern system from five separate entrances.

"I guess it's time for us to get ready," said Becky. "You know, when I said I wanted to be a pilot, fighting in an alien space war wasn't exactly what I had in mind."

"Yeah. Reporter might be a safer profession right about now," I said.

"Right now, I'd settle for plain old seventh grader. Don't tell Hollins, but I'm completely terrified."

"Well, growing up is doing what you have to do. Even when you're afraid," I offered.

"Where did you get that?" asked Becky. "Seriously, Chorkle. That's the cheesiest thing I've ever heard in my life."

Becky and I walked toward her newly modified starfighter. On the nose of her ship, the glowing tetrahedron of the Q-sik spun slowly. The device had been connected to special controls inside. Kalac stood and stared at it.

"Chorkle, please translate for Becky," said my originator. "To break through that battle cruiser's energy shields, I will be using a higher power setting for the Q-sik. After we aim it, it will take at least a minute to spin up to its greatest speed before it can fire." I repeated this in human. Becky nodded.

This was the nearest I'd been to the Q-sik yet. I could feel the power radiating from it in dizzying waves. The closer I got, the more my skin tingled. It felt like passing through the Stealth Shield times a hundred.

"Firing this weapon brings unintended consequences," said Kalac. "I realize that now. The only thing worse than using it again would be letting the Vorem have it."

I hoped that was true. After all, this whole thing had been my idea. "It's not too late," I said. "Maybe we could destroy the Q-sik instead. That way, no one could ever use it again."

"I think that was Jalasu Jhuk's ultimate goal," said Kalac. "It left such extensive notes on the Q-sik not so that we would know how to use it as a weapon but to help one day destroy it."

"So does the manual explain how?"

"No. Apparently Jhuk never figured it out. Otherwise it would have done so a long time ago," said Kalac. "According to Jhuk's notes, damaging the Q-sik in any way could release the energy contained within. When we fire it—when you see its power—you'll understand just how catastrophic that would be."

"Kalac, I don't understand. If Xotonians didn't create the Q-sik, and the Vorem didn't either . . . then who did?"

Kalac shook its head. "The manual offers no clue. It seems we're all starting to realize that there is much in the universe that we don't know. It makes what is certain all the more valuable. . . ."

"What do you mean?"

"Chorkle . . . I'm so sorry I said I wished I'd never originated you. It was a lie."

"I know," I said.

"Originating you was the greatest thing I ever did," said Kalac. And it hugged me close. Tears welled in all of our eyes.

At last, Kalac nodded. It turned and boarded the star-fighter. Becky cleared her throat. She'd been standing beside us the whole time.

"Wow, you Xotonians sure get emotional," said Becky. "I can't imagine how much you're going to blubber at their wedding." She pointed at Nicki and Hollins. They stood together on the other side of the hangar, laughing.

"Seriously, though," said Becky. "Good for those crazy kids." She was smiling.

"Wait, what? Oh. But I thought you and Hollins, uh . . ." I said. Human interpersonal dynamics were still mysterious to me. Becky's in particular.

"Chorkle, gross," she said simply. And she boarded the ship. I followed her.

Becky flopped down in the cockpit and adjusted the seat. Hollins's face appeared on the com screen. He was in the other ship now, and Nicki stood behind him.

"You guys ready?" he said. "Let's do this and then go home." His voice was calm, and his face was serious.

"Just so I understand the 'plan'—and I'm using that term loosely," said Becky, "two children are going to fly a couple of ancient spaceships against an evil alien empire of untold power. Is that it?"

"Yeah, I think that about covers it," said Hollins.

"One heck of a college entrance essay," said Becky as she powered up the engines. "FYI, I'm just going to ignore about eighty percent of this stuff." She indicated the ridiculously complicated array of meters and displays on the instrument panel. Even after working with the ships for the past day, there was still much about the ships we didn't understand.

"Maybe we can figure out the rest of it later," said Nicki cheerfully, "if we don't die."

"You're a real ray of sunshine, sis," laughed Becky. She seemed oddly lighthearted to be only minutes from risking her life in an incredibly dangerous flight mission.

"Wait," I said, suddenly gripped with panic. "We can't do this. There's no way it will work! It's impossible—"

"Chorkle, it's not impossible," said Nicki. "'Believe you can, and you're halfway there.' Didn't Teddy Roosevelt say that, Hollins?"

"Yeah, I—I think he did," said Hollins, his eyes wide with admiration. "I didn't know you were into T. R. quotes."

Nicki shrugged and smiled.

Becky rolled her eyes. "Okay. Can we please just fight the Vorem before I throw up? You good, Chorkle?"

I tried to say something, but no words would come out.

"I choose to interpret your silence as a yes," said Becky.

Ghillen appeared on the com screen. "Opening the

hangar bay now," said the Observer. High above us came a creaking mechanical noise. The hinges of the massive doors slowly swung outward with a rush of air.

I took my seat in the blaster turret as the ship lifted upward on vertical thrusters. The starfighter containing Hollins and Nicki floated up beside us.

Kalac took the controls of the Q-sik in its thol'grazes. "Ack'cer dor," said my originator. Xotonian for "good luck."

CHAPTER THIRTY-FOUR

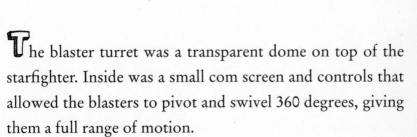

The blaster turret was a transparent dome on top of the starfighter. Inside was a small com screen and controls that allowed the blasters to pivot and swivel 360 degrees, giving them a full range of motion.

This transparent bubble offered an amazing vantage point as we rose out of the gravitational field of the asteroid. The surface of Gelo diminished beneath us. T'utzuxe grew larger, and the glittering void of space lay beyond it, calm and cold and beautiful.

I tried not to throw up.

"Go time," said Hollins's voice over the radio. "Nicki and I will hit the ones on the ground. Fly by once and hopefully take them all out, quick. You go for that cruiser."

"Got it," said Becky. "Or 'roger.' Whatever." Becky whirled our ship. Ahead of us, in the distance, Ridian's battle cruiser now loomed. The Observers' telescopes had not done it justice—it was somehow even bigger and more threatening than they'd made it seem. Triremes flitted around it like angry insects. Every instinct I had said we ought to be moving away from that black engine of death, fleeing as fast as we could.

Instead Becky said, "Hang on." And she punched the forward thrusters. We were flying right at it.

I spun the turret and looked back toward Gelo. Some distance behind us, Hollins was flying his fighter low and fast across the surface, coming up on a landed trireme. Nicki began to fire green bolts of energy from her own turret, strafing the ground.

The Vorem were unprepared for this, surprised that we possessed any ships at all. We had to take advantage of it while we could.

One of the triremes on the surface flew to pieces as it silently bloomed in flame.

"Got one!" crackled Nicki over the radio.

"Nice shooting, Nicki!" I cried.

"Wait, got two more," said Nicki. Down on Gelo, more explosions.

"Chorkle," cried Becky, "pay attention. We've got incom—"

Our ship shook as we took fire from one of the triremes protecting the battle cruiser. They'd seen us now, and they were beginning to coordinate a response.

The trireme was flying right for us, leading with a hail of red lasers. I spun the turret around and began to shoot. Another blast took a chunk out of our ship.

"We're hit. Something's beeping," said Becky. "I hope it's not important."

As I started to fire, the trireme peeled off and began evasive maneuvers, weaving and rolling and changing its direction.

And somehow, I just couldn't hit it. Wherever I shot, the trireme was no longer there. These Vorem ships were incredibly agile or their pilots were incredibly skilled—or both. My Xenostrife skills were coming up short.

"Come on, Chorkle," said Becky.

"It's a lot harder than the game!" I said.

"It's not a game," said Becky.

I stopped firing for a moment and tracked the Vorem ship's zigzagging progress now. I took a deep breath. Then, instead of firing where the ship was, I fired where it would be.

The trireme burst in a flash of light.

"Nice!" yelled Becky.

I replied with one of the human expletives that I'd been told to use sparingly. Two more Vorem ships were now between the battle cruiser and us, flying right at us in tight formation and shooting all the while. Their laser blasts whizzed past the turret, half a meter from my head.

"They don't want to let us at the battle cruiser," I said.

"Don't worry," said Becky. "We can get past them. I've done this before. . . ." And she punched the thrusters, hard. The force of the acceleration pressed me back in my seat. We were hurtling toward the two triremes at high speed now.

"Of course, when I did it before," said Becky, "it was on a rocket-bike."

"Has the human gone crazy?" cried Kalac, staring out the viewport. "Chorkle, what is she doing?"

"Jalasu Jhuk help us," I said, "I think I know."

Any moment now we were going to smash right into the two triremes. There was no longer time to decelerate or turn aside, even if Becky had wanted to. And she didn't want to.

There would be a crash. An explosion. Perhaps we would all meet again—Xotonian, Vorem, and human alike—in the Nebula Beyond. I braced for impact.

"Let's see Hollins do this," said Becky.

At that moment, she rolled the starfighter—wider than

it was tall—onto its side. Time seemed to slow to a crawl. Our ship scraped right between the two triremes.

Becky had repeated her move from Jehe Canyon. Only instead of a rocket-bike, she'd used a starfighter. And instead of boulders, it had been Vorem starships fixated on our destruction.

From my vantage point on top of the starfighter—which was now the side—I could clearly see one of the Vorem pilots in his cockpit. As we hurtled past, he threw his arms up in slow motion, an expression of terror or anger or admiration. Perhaps some combination of all three.

I whipped the turret around backward and put three holes right in his engine. His trireme powered down, trailing black smoke.

Now there was nothing between us and the battle cruiser.

"I've got two on my tail, and I can't seem to get rid of them," crackled Hollins's voice. I spun and saw Hollins and Nicki's ship coming toward us with two triremes close behind, the two that they hadn't destroyed on the surface. The triremes must have taken off and followed Hollins back.

I looked for a shot, but I couldn't find one—not without accidentally shooting my friends.

Just then, one of the pursuers exploded. Nicki had nailed

him! But their fighter was still taking heavy fire from the other. The starfighter spewed smoke and flames.

The battle cruiser was just ahead of us now, massive and foreboding. I spun the turret toward it and began to shoot. The lasers made small scorch marks wherever they hit, here and there dislodging a piece of metal or machinery. It seemed an almost futile gesture.

"All right, this is it," said Kalac. "Powering up the Q-sik." And my originator did. Even in the midst of the battle, I felt something different, some change in fundamental particle flow around us. The Q-sik seemed to pull energy toward it.

"How many triremes left?" said Becky, snapping me back to reality. "Three? Four?"

I wasn't sure. In the chaos, I'd lost count. There was still the one we'd flown past and one following Hollins and—

Two more triremes flew at us from above, pounding our ship with laser fire. Our starfighter rocked and sparks leaped from the consoles. More beeping. Louder this time. Oily smoke began to fill the interior.

"I think we lost an engine!" cried Becky.

I spun the turret upward and fired on the two ships. But when I pulled the trigger, nothing happened.

"They must have hit something important. The blasters

are dead. No power," I said. The two triremes continued their punishing barrage of lasers. Becky was flying evasively, but with one engine down, the ship was sluggish and unresponsive. We were getting hit. Hard.

"I think—I think I'm done over here," said Hollins over the radio. Apparently Nicki had taken out another Vorem in the meantime, but their starfighter was also heavily damaged. It tumbled senselessly under the force of its own momentum. One of its engines fired sporadically. Still the remaining trireme kept on shooting at it.

Worst of all, it seemed that the crew of the battle cruiser had finally realized what was happening—that they were under attack. Slowly, the massive ship wheeled to face us.

"When is that Q-sik going to fire?" screamed Nicki. She was struggling to keep the nose of the ship aimed at the battle cruiser.

Though it seemed the length of a lifetime, we'd been in the air for all of three, maybe four, minutes. And now everything was coming apart.

"I'm sorry," I said.

The plan was never going to work. After all, we were only children, Xotonian and human children. I'd just wanted to help them get back to their parents. But somehow we'd all ended up fighting a war, trying to alter the course of history.

In a way, it was impressive that we'd even come this close. We'd taken out seven of the ten triremes. We'd almost fired the Q-sik. We'd nearly saved Gelo and Eo.

We'd done our best. Better than anyone could have expected. But we'd been defeated. Both of our ships were defenseless now, rapidly being shot to pieces by the Vorem. The gun batteries of the battle cruiser had turned—now they were firing on us too. We'd be destroyed before the Q-sik could fire. It was never going to work. It was impossible.

"Goodbye, Kalac," I said.

"Goodbye, Chorkle. I love you."

Ridian would have the Q-sik. The Vorem would have Gelo. And Earth. None of us would make it back to our homes. I thought of Linod and Commander Hollins and Hudka and Little Gus.

Little Gus. I could almost hear his voice coming over the radio. . . .

"Yo. Miss me, dudes?"

From out of the corner of my fifth eye, I saw a flash—one of the wings had been blown off the Vorem trireme that was attacking Hollins's ship. A greenish blur was coming in fast.

"What the hell?" said Becky.

It was the third starfighter! Suddenly, two of the battle cruiser's gun batteries exploded to bits in a hail of laser fire.

"Little Gus is the original king!" he screamed over the radio. His ship swooped around. Now he was flying right at the last two triremes, lasers blazing. Whoever was in that blaster turret was an amazing shot. As I thought this, I realized who it must be.

"Exciting, isn't it, Chorkle? I feel positively young," cried Hudka. "Like I'm a hundred seventy-two all over again!" My grand-originator gave a salute—still shooting—as they whizzed past. One of the triremes attacking us burst into a cloud of fire and glass and shards of black metal. Only one left now.

"Little Gus," cried Hollins, "how did you—"

"We followed you. Had to knock down a couple of Observers to get into the ship," said Little Gus. "Worth it! Now you have to admit that I am the greatest pilot that ever—"

And Little Gus crashed his starfighter right into the final trireme, sending both spacecraft spinning.

"Crap! How do you stop these things?" asked Gus. "No brake pedal!"

More gun batteries on the battle cruiser turned to fire on us.

"C'mon!" screamed Becky, fighting with the control stick. "When is this thing going to—"

"It is ready," said Kalac. There was fear in my originator's voice.

CHAPTER THIRTY-FIVE

The universe began to vibrate. The stars and the planets and the ship and the atoms of my body shook. And just when everything seemed as though it might fly apart into its constituent subparticles—

All was white—or something brighter than white. A nameless shade, so bright I'd never seen it before. So bright that I knew it would be burned into my memory forever. For an instant or an age, this whiteness lasted. I closed all five of my eyes and clapped my thol'grazes over my face. This had no effect.

When at last I opened them again, I saw a cone of pure, radiant energy firing from the nose of our ship.

This beam of light cut through the battle cruiser—shredded the hulk of black metal as easily as if it were a particularly complex paper model. No, more easily than that.

It was as though, to the light, the battle cruiser didn't exist. And if we had pointed the Q-sik at something else—an asteroid or a planet or even a star—the light would have cut through it just the same. Somehow I knew this.

Behind the cruiser, space itself seemed to bend and warp where the Q-sik had fired. Punched inward like a sheet of taut rubber.

This was what Jalasu Jhuk was trying to protect the universe from. The weapon to end all weapons. In the wrong hands, it could create destruction on an incomprehensible scale. Perhaps even in the right hands?

At this moment it struck me that we didn't even know the full extent of its powers. Ridian had called it the "Universe Ender," and as I saw its power, I believed him.

And I knew that as long as the Q-sik existed, we would be tempted to use it.

CHAPTER THIRTY-SIX

"Holy . . . crap," said Gus over the radio. I blinked as the glow of the Q-sik faded from my eyes. Out past the battle cruiser, the vortex of warped space still shimmered. It looked like the sky had been . . . punctured.

"We did it," said Becky.

"By Jalasu Jhuk," said Kalac, though I couldn't tell if he spoke in triumph or horror.

Nearly half of the battle cruiser was gone. Just gone. Burned away cleanly. What was left of the hulk spun oddly; most guidance and propulsion systems had surely been disabled or destroyed by the blast. None of its gun batteries moved.

The final trireme was flying back toward the crippled battle cruiser now. Retreating.

"What about that last one?" asked Little Gus.

"Let it go," said Hollins. "We've beaten them."

"You must have disabled their communications systems!" radioed Ydar. "They're no longer jamming surface transmissions."

"Can you contact the *Phryxus*?" I said.

"Just a moment," said Ydar. "Yes, I see the human ships. They're not far now, less than a hundred thousand kilometers from Gelo. Okay, patching them through to you." The High Observer punched some controls off screen.

Now the com screen showed Commander Hollins. "Danny! Kids!" she said. "Are you safe?"

"Define 'safe,'" said Becky.

"Yeah, we're all fine," said Hollins.

"Kids, we detected a massive energy spike and several— well, they look like spacecraft, near 48172-Rybar. Do you know what's going on there?"

"It's over now, Mom," laughed Hollins. "We won. We beat them. And the asteroid isn't called 'Rybar.' It's Gelo."

"And these aliens—these 'Xotonians'—haven't hurt you?"

"Does the oog-ball match count?" asked Nicki quietly.

"No," said Hollins. "They haven't hurt us. In fact, I think they may have just helped us save Earth."

"Well, that's—that's good," said Commander Hollins.

"Look, we'll be landing on the asteroid in two hours. We're going to bring you all home." She was openly crying now.

"Sure, Mom," said young Hollins. "I can't wait."

"Commander Hollins," said Becky, "can you tell my mom and dad something for me?"

"Yes, Rebecca, anything," she said.

"Can you tell them I want a car?" she said. "A nice one."

"Me too," said Nicki.

"I'll tell them," said Commander Hollins.

"You know, I'll take one too," said Little Gus, "if the Garcías are just giving them out."

"Okay. I will relay that message to them, Augustus," laughed Commander Hollins. "You have my word."

"I love you, Mom," said Hollins.

"I love you too. I'm never letting you out of my sight again until you're thirty-five."

"We'll see you in two hours," said Hollins. "Hollins out." And the transmission ended.

"We're all going home," said Nicki.

"Maybe. If I can get us back to Gelo in one piece," said Becky. Our damaged starfighter lurched as she steered it slowly back toward my asteroid. "Hollins, can you fly?"

"Yeah," he said. "It'll be slow going for us, though. We were hit pretty hard. I've only got one engine, and it keeps cutting out." I could see his ship from the turret. It was in bad shape, full of blaster holes. But it was moving.

"Okay, but can you fly?" said Becky again. "Like, do you actually know how to fly?"

"Ha ha," said Hollins.

"Wait, what is happening?" said Kalac, suddenly staring out the viewport. The shimmering vortex of bent space seemed to be growing. The battle cruiser pathetically fired the few engines it had left. It was no use. The giant ship began to tumble out of its orbit. It was slowly falling toward the light.

Once more Ydar came over the com screen. "I'm detecting a surge of dark energy just beyond Gelo."

"What?" I said. "What does that mean?"

"A wormhole," whispered Kalac. "We created a—"

"Gravity looks like it's spiking!" screamed Ydar. "You need to get out of there!"

"Something's pulling me," said Hollins as their ship tumbled past us.

Becky punched the thrusters. But even as we flew toward Gelo, the wormhole grew closer. It was sucking us in.

But how could we be moving toward two things at once? Suddenly, it dawned on me. We weren't moving toward Gelo. The asteroid was hurtling toward us. It was being drawn into the wormhole too!

"Can't. Get. Free . . ." growled Becky. And at last, our ship fell into the glowing vortex.

Once more, all was white. Whiter than white. I felt like I couldn't breathe, like I was being crushed and infinitely stretched in every direction at once. I was freezing cold and boiling hot.

And then, suddenly, we weren't where we were.

CHAPTER THIRTY-SEVEN

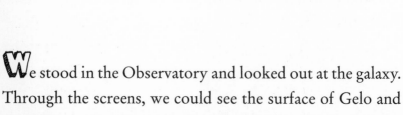

We stood in the Observatory and looked out at the galaxy. Through the screens, we could see the surface of Gelo and space beyond it. The stars shone brightly in the blackness.

But they were different stars now.

The disabled battle cruiser hung in the sky too. A broken hulk traveling the same orbital path as Gelo, unable to move under its own force. Still, its red lights blinked.

There were other, less subtle changes to our sky as well. T'utxuze the Red Planet was gone. Instead, Gelo now orbited a green planet that the Observers had yet to identify.

This new world was covered in soaring mountains and dense, lush forests and oceans of salty water. Preliminary scans seemed to indicate that it was inhabited. By whom? At this point, that was anyone's guess.

We had traversed a wormhole. According to Nicki and Ydar, the power of the Q-sik's blast had ripped a hole in the fabric of space-time. This rip had temporarily connected two distant points in the universe.

But unlike the tiny, short-lived wormhole created when the Q-sik was first fired, the second one was large and stable enough to pull an entire asteroid through—before sealing itself forever.

Gelo had been spit out somewhere . . . else. And so far, none of our ancient star-maps had provided any clue as to where.

We had beaten the Vorem, though. Inside the tunnels, the fighting had been fierce. There were many Xotonian casualties, and the attackers had pressed all the way to Core-of-Rock. Parts of the city had been badly damaged. But when the battle cruiser was disabled, the Vorem lost their will to fight. The Vorem legion had surrendered—or most of them had, anyway. They were now being held prisoner. The legate in command of the invasion, however, had yet to be captured.

We had kept the Q-sik from our enemies. Gelo was unconquered (if relocated). And Earth was safe. Against all odds, we had won.

"You acted with such bravery. We all owe you a debt of

gratitude," said Kalac in halting human—my originator was starting to pick up the language.

"We are pretty great, aren't we?" said Little Gus, holding Pizza in his arms. The other Xotonians in the room eyed the thyss-cat nervously, their skin instinctively camouflaged.

"What's the Xotonian equivalent of a Ferrari?" asked Becky. "Because I think we deserve it."

"Come on," said Hollins. "We didn't do it for material reward."

"It's probably an usk-lizard, anyway," said Nicki.

"Huh," said Becky. "Maybe I'll pass then."

Nicki looked out at the strange planet we now orbited and the swirling galaxies beyond. She shook her head. "You know, we could be anywhere in the universe. Fascinating."

"Sis, you and I have a very different definition of 'fascinating,'" said Becky.

"Seriously, though," said Nicki, "we could be one light-year from Earth. Or a hundred thousand. Both distances are still so astronomically huge, they're practically the same thing. I mean, even if we had the fastest human spaceship, it would still take us nearly two hundred fifty years to travel even one light-year. And that's if we even knew which direction to go. . . ." As she noticed the other humans staring at her, she stopped thinking out loud.

"What I mean is that it will be an adventure," said Nicki, smiling.

"That's for sure," said Hollins. "But we can do it. We will do it. We helped save two worlds. I think we can find our way back home."

"At least now I really will get to skip seventh grade," said Becky. "Suck it, Mrs. Pascarella."

"I'm just happy that I'm here with my best friend," said Gus, tickling Pizza's belly. "And my second-best friend, of course." He clapped me on the back. "For the record, Hollins, you and Nicki are tied for third place. And, Becky, you're, like, my nineteenth best friend."

"Please, tell me how I can get to twentieth," said Becky.

"Well," I said, "you all may not be able to get back to your own homes yet, but you can certainly come to ours." Kalac nodded and placed a thol'graz on mine.

We descended all five thousand spiraling steps of Dynusk's Column and stepped out into the glittering underground city.

There, before us, a huge crowd had gathered. I saw Loghoz and Dyves and Glyac; Ornim and Chayl and Eromu; even old Gatas had come. Plus countless more Xotonians that I knew, many bearing the wounds of the recent battle. For a long moment, they stared at us in silence.

Somewhere, a voice called out a single word: "Human!"

It was Linod, I realized. Somehow it had pushed its way to the front. Again it called out, "Human!" And it pumped its spindly thol'grazes in the air.

And this time, the crowd took up the chant: "Human! Human! Human!"

I chanted it too.

And they followed us, cheering, across Ryzz Plaza, past the Vault and the Hall of Wonok, all the way back to my home.

There, Hudka invited as many inside as would fit. We ate Xotonian burritos and played Xenostryfe III. I even gave out Feeney's Original Astronaut Ice Cream bars for dessert.